THE CURSE OF THE ARCADIAN STONE

THE CURSE OF THE ARCADIAN STONE

S. R. BREAKER

Contents

"I found you once. I can find you again."
-an idiot boy to his dragon girl

Prologue

It always starts the same.

I'm being chased, but I never know by whom.

My lungs burn. My legs are lead.

Biting, cold air whooshes around me as I stop short in a secluded clearing before a frozen lake.

A silvery haze drifts across the lake's surface, swirling in the dim light. It veils the ice in a shroud, as if guarding ancient secrets beneath its layers of frost.

As if it had done so for thousands of years.

When I look up, she's there, standing by the top of the tallest tree.

Silhouetted by the glow of dusk.

Her long, wild pink hair nearly blends into the sky.

Intoxicating jasmine and cypress tickle my nose as I gasp in air.

But my heart still pounds in my ears. I can barely hear my own heavy breathing.

She's in danger.

I need to take her away from here.

I need to save her.

She reaches her hand out, as if she's calling for me, as if she knows me...

I can almost get a clear glimpse of her face as a dense white mist blows in, and the world spins in a dizzying panorama.

Suddenly, I'm back in the city, walking home from work.

Except there's something wrong with my usual shortcut through the alley. The graffiti on the walls looks as if they are in motion. The narrow walkway squeezes me in. Shadows lean in and fold, whispering a touch, but then recede.

Before I could even blink at the hint of sparkles of light a few feet away, a brilliant, not-quite-liquid silvery sphere bursts to life with a crackle right before my already widened eyes.

An ominous chill crawls up my skin, but as my mouth drops open in awe, a shock of a bright pink figure shoots out of the sphere and crashes into me.

Then the thick fog blows in once more, obscuring everything.

And the dream leaves me.

***

1

Chapter One - A Dream

With a slow breath, I roused from the lingering depths of sleep.

Right outside my window, metal tracks groaned and clanked under the weight of the BMT rail transit line train as it loudly rumbled past.

I'd already grown accustomed to the noise since moving here some years back, to the smallest one-bedroom apartment ever in Brooklyn.

Having not bothered to open my eyes, I lay still in bed.

The few framed photos I had on the windowsill rattled ever so slightly, along with what few pieces of furniture I owned. The vibrations rolling through the building faded into the distance, leaving the handful of urgent shouts, clacking of hurried footfalls, and chattering filtering up from the streets below my second-floor apartment as the city stirred to life with its usual Thursday morning routine.

But despite the bright light seeping in through my eyelids, I wasn't at all eager to check in with reality just yet.

I was still bathed in that scent from my dreams—fragrant cypress and jasmine.

I'd always thought that dream fragments were supposed to fade away once you woke up. Most people weren't even able to remember their dreams at all. But for some reason, my dreams from the past few months had remained as vivid to me while I was awake as they were when I was asleep.

Always of the same forest, the same girl. That last part, in the city, was new though.

I'd already seen a shrink.

She reckoned it could just be residual trauma from that 'episode' I'd had when I was seventeen. When it seemed as though I'd lost an entire week's worth of memories. But I was much younger then, much more confused.

My mom called what had happened to me a 'nervous breakdown', attributing it to the stress I'd been under at the time, struggling with multiple odd jobs to help keep the family afloat through our unfortunate circumstances.

Except something in my gut told me it was more than that.

It had to be.

I just couldn't remember.

I rubbed my face with one hand, groaning when the slight movement sent a stinging strain up my arm. My muscles ached as if I'd spent all of yesterday carrying sacks of cement, like when I'd volunteered to build houses for charity two years ago, or when I thought I would train for that city-wide marathon, but ended up nearly injured instead.

What the hell did I do last night? Had I gone drinking with the guys after work? My sister's birthday party wasn't until tonight. I was sure it wasn't some kind of hangover—

Wait a minute.

There was something on my leg. I couldn't move it. I couldn't move my other arm either, and when I tried to move again, there was a soft moan.

I froze.

What the—?

Already dreading opening my eyes, I peeked out of one, and almost stopped breathing.

The top of a head of long, silky pink hair was on my pillow.

There was someone else in my bed.

Heck—there was a *girl* in my bed.

I caught my breath again as the events of last night finally slammed right back into my brain.

Holy...

I scrambled to jump out of bed, dragging the muddy bedsheets with me.

Except, she was also tangled in the sheets, so when I got up, she rolled right off the bed with a yelp and a loud thump.

Okay...she sounds pretty non-imaginary.

I winced. "Oh, shoot—s-sorry!" Swallowing hard, I warily watched the top of that fiery pink-haired head rising up from behind the mattress. "A-are you okay?"

When that piercing violet gaze met mine, it didn't let go even as she stood upright.

But I couldn't stop staring.

Her long tunic sleeveless dress was rumpled. I could tell it used to be multi-colored but it was generously splattered with mud. The daylight streaming in through the windows silhouetted her form, with her pale skin and bright hair making it look as if she was glowing. She was clearly livid—eyebrows furrowed, lips pursed thin, but somehow the fierce expression on her face only made her more enigmatic and mysterious.

She was as incredibly beautiful as I remembered.

Except she was here, for real, standing in front of me.

The girl from my dreams.

Or—check that...no longer a girl, but a young woman.

My heart pounded in my chest as what had started as excitement turned into dread.

Damn. So yesterday *was* real.

Discreetly glancing down, I was relieved I was still completely dressed—which meant that, at least, I hadn't done anything last night which I would no doubt very quickly regret.

Only, my generic consultant work clothes were just as mud-splattered as hers.

I blinked at the recollection.

Because there happened to be a mud puddle in the alley yesterday.

In front of the honest-to-god swirling portal she had tumbled out of—before sprawling onto me and knocking us both to the ground.

A small part of me wanted to turn on the skepticism and disbelief on full blast.

Portals weren't real. Magic wasn't real. Santa Claus sure as shooting wasn't real.

But I'd seen that brilliant blue tear in the world with my own eyes.

And somehow, I knew, deep inside—I already knew what she was.

I took another long breath. "Are you...from another world?"

She cocked her head to one side ever so slightly, still regarding me with that sharp look. For a moment, I wondered if she didn't understand English, but then she finally responded. "Yes."

Her soft, steady voice shot an unexpected thrill up my spine.

In the dreams, I'd never heard her speak. But hearing her voice for the first time somehow fulfilled a strange longing I'd never even realized was there. It was almost as if...as if I missed her.

Except for obviously, I'd never met her before.

She shifted her eyes from mine to assess the room—the single bed with the sheets in total disarray, the plain blue curtains, the small corner desk, the framed photos. Her cautious gaze stopped curiously at the 'Hang in there' cat poster behind me taped to the wall for a long moment, before wandering some more.

She took a slow step sideways to walk around the bed, moving as if toward me. "Is this...the fourth realm?"

My eyebrows shot up. "Um..." I scratched my head. "I guess that could be what your people call this world."

The scents of the sweet forest swirled in the air again as she approached. Mesmerized by her beauty, her mere presence, I was frozen where I stood. I didn't want to move in case this was all a dream and she would disappear if I did. But this *had* to be a dream. And if it was, this would be the most vivid of all of my dreams of her so far.

Before I knew what was going on, she launched herself at me, tackling me back down onto the bed.

"What the—?" My eyes widened in surprise, even wider when she began to hurriedly unbutton my shirt. "Whoa, hey wait—!"

The girl whom I'd been dreaming of for months was on top of me in my own bed and taking my clothes off. My mind whirled even as I tried to push her hands away.

But her eyebrows were furrowed in determination—and for some reason, she was bloody strong!

After a few buttons, she tugged my shirt open, her eyes darting up and down over my bare chest. Stopping short altogether, her frown deepened.

She let out a forceful breath, before mumbling, as if to herself. "It's not here."

Completely disoriented, I glanced down at myself. "What?"

Breathless, her suspicious violet gaze met mine again. "Who are you? Why don't you have the mark?"

Struggling to sit up, I tempered my aggravated yell to an exasperated hiss. "For god's sake, was that absolutely necessary?"

There was a loud knocking at the door and my gaze snapped up.

"Josh!" the screechy yell was muffled.

My heart jumped to my throat. *Oh, shoot.* I looked over at the pink-haired girl again, and then down at my lap where she was straddling me, then at my shirt gaping wide open.

Uh-oh.

2

Chapter Two - Stranger

Alarm clear in my voice, I scrambled to straighten up. "That's my sister, Erin." I tried to push the girl off, but she tightened her arms around my neck.

Her head quirking to one side again, she studied my reaction, likely registering my panic.

I shot her a weird look. "What are you doing? Get off. You need to hide!"

'Mystery girl' pursed her lips. "Only if you vow to help me."

What? My jaw nearly dropped.

"Josh, come on!" The knocking at the door got more insistent.

Her steely violet gaze settled on me again. "Swear an oath to me and I will comply."

I cringed in frustration. I really couldn't let my sister walk in on me with a girl on my lap like this, but what the hell was she talking about—an oath?

"Josh, open up or I'm using the spare keys Mom gave me—" Loud jingling filtered through the door. I guessed Erin had completely decided to ignore the 'privacy' rule we'd agreed on, and totally forgot what 'for emergency purposes' meant.

"Erin, for the love of—just wait!" I hollered back before meeting the girl's expectant gaze again. Her grip around my shoulders was tightening again. Closing my eyes for a moment, I blew out a breath. "What oath? What do you need me to do?"

"It's just a small errand," she assured with not even a hitch in her tone. "There is someone in this realm I need to find. I am told they should be very close to this location, and I have—"

"Fine!" I stood up with a soft grunt, carrying her aloft with me, before striding toward the closet across the room to shake her off. "I swear I will do everything I can to help you find whoever you want to find, now just get down, get in the closet, and shush!"

I had shut the door to the closet with a whoosh just as my nosy sister Erin sauntered through the doorway, twirling the keys around her fingers.

Pausing there, Erin made a face at the state of my seemingly ransacked bedroom. "Jeez, and here I thought I was the messy one."

Jumping in alert, I went to pull the muddy sheets off the bed altogether before going around to tidy up. Still a bit breathless, I ran my fingers through my hair to counter, "Nobody asked for your opinion, Erin. Also, why are you in my apartment?"

She gave me a critical look up and down. "What on earth happened to you? Don't you have work today? You're all muddy."

Already annoyed, I rebuttoned my shirt. "None of your business." Stuffing the dirty sheets in the laundry basket, I glanced over my shoulder at her. "I think I want my emergency key back. This isn't high school anymore, Erin. You can't just barge into my room and steal my stuff whenever you want."

Headed straight for my bureau, she stuck her tongue out at me. "Oh, whatever. I'm just here to rummage for decorations for my birthday party. I'm doing a 90s theme. Hey—" She pointed an old Walkman at me. "You better make sure you come tonight." Her eyes glinted in mischief. "I think Mom's setting you up with some girl again."

Groaning, I rubbed my face with my hand. "I told her she needs to stop doing this. It's like she doesn't even hear me when I explain. I don't need help finding a girlfriend. Never have, never will. Or—" I cringed. "Just because I haven't had a relationship in years doesn't make it a crisis that needs to be fixed."

Erin waved her had to dismiss it. "If you say so. Or else you'd have to call in to your own office's 'Crisis Management' department, and you'd have to answer the call."

"We'll see if work isn't busy today." I gave a half-hearted shrug.

She wrinkled her nose. "Didn't you get fired yet? I thought you hated that job anyway?"

I shot her a mock offended look. "I don't hate it. I just...can't stand my boss, and my colleagues, and...the work."

Not bothering to look at me, her shoulders shook with mirth. "Josh, you are twenty-five years old. You seriously need to figure out what you want to do with your life. Unless your dream really is to answer customer complaint calls all day long." Sighing, she dropped more of my stuff into a tote bag. "Sometimes I feel like I'm the older one here. It's just like Mom keeps saying. You are so talented in so many things, but you have absolutely no direction. And it's only gotten worse since..." she trailed off.

I already knew what she was going to say.

Back when I'd had my 'episode', everyone figured it was triggered by the fact that my dad had also recently died.

My mom and Erin had been pretty distraught at the time too. Though I was sure what I'd felt was a bit of a relief. Perhaps my underlying devastation must have simply had a worse impact on me than I'd wanted to believe.

Frank Richards had *not* been a shining example of fatherhood. He was always busy, mostly out of the house, as though we, his family, were nothing but an inconvenience for him. I'd never understood why my mom couldn't find it in herself to leave him.

Nowadays, my mom was settled into a good job at the bank and seeing a new guy who had already proven himself a reliable and stand-up sort of fellow. Erin was a year out of college and doing well. I hadn't been to my shrink in months.

Still, we had all successfully put everything behind us and I was grateful that my family had made it through those rough times.

It was history.

"Alright, alright." With another dismissive wave, I moved to shove her out the door, even as she tried to shuffle back against me in vain. "Thanks for the pep talk and you'd better give back all of my stuff after the party."

Erin merely stuck her tongue out at me again, yelling out, "Make sure you're there tonight. You know you don't want to disappoint Mom!" before whirling around to leave voluntarily.

Once the door slammed shut, I blew out a huge breath and collapsed onto the bed.

Jeez. I rubbed my face with my hand. That was close.

It was true that my mom had been on my case, setting me up with potential girlfriends—mostly daughters of her friends from Pilates. Most of them were nice enough, but I'd always maintained that I wasn't looking for a relationship because I was much too busy with work.

The last thing I needed was for Erin to report that I was already secretly cavorting with one in my apartment.

I shot the closed closet door a dirty look.

Swear an oath to me and I will comply.

What a manipulative little shrew. I should have known this woman was going to cause me nothing but trouble.

Standing up again, I walked to the closet. Bracing my hand on the knob, I stopped with a momentary notion.

Maybe she wouldn't be there. Maybe I had only imagined that whole thing. Maybe I was just overwhelmed with work again and having traumatic flashbacks from that episode years ago that I had simply hallucinated the girl from my dreams.

Peeking inside, I opened the door, but that familiar fragrance wafting out was already an easy giveaway.

This girl was real.

She was awkwardly hunched against the rack since I had sort of unceremoniously dropped her in there. She was a burst of color in my closet—her wild, pink hair in full contrast against my mostly black pants and white shirts on hangers.

Those incensed violet eyes lifted to meet mine again. "Was that absolutely necessary?" The timbre of her voice had darkened, and somehow, an invisible wind was beginning to whirl around in my room. A smoky hazy glow emanated from her form, from her eyes.

It took an effort for my jaw not to drop. I wanted to blink profusely to make sure I wasn't seeing things, but my eyes were permanently stunned wide.

Talk about 'out of the frying pan and into the fire.'

I swallowed my nerves. "Um, sorry about that," I dismissed with a wave, offering her my hand, before she exploded altogether or something. "You can come out now."

She gave me an up-and-down assessing look—for who knew what reason, since obviously *she* was the more dangerous one between the two of us. But she seemed to reach the same conclusion. The glow surrounding her dissipated, the inexplicable wind died down.

Though still wary, the girl took my hand to straighten up and took a step forward.

Right then, I was struck again with that overwhelmingly familiar sensation.

Why did I already feel closer to her than any other girl I'd previously met? Something about her being here set me immediately at ease. Maybe it was because I'd been dreaming about her for months, sure, but it was as if...there was something else, something more... What was it?

Without thinking, I gently stroked her hand with my thumb. A tingling ran up the length of my arm. "Have we met before?"

She held my gaze for a moment. I was almost certain she was having the same strange sense of familiarity, even as she seemed to also strain to remember.

I almost held my breath, waiting for her response.

But when she blinked to avert her gaze, the moment broke. She pulled her hand away to step well back from me.

Straightening up, I cleared my throat.

Her gaze flicked to my face then down to my muddy clothes. She looked down at herself. "I must get cleaned up."

3

Chapter Three - Too Late

'It's like rain or a waterfall', I'd had to explain after turning on the shower for her.

The girl's face had been entirely blank. It could have been annoyance for my mansplaining, but it could have also been that she'd honestly never seen a shower before in her entire life, but she didn't want to seem daunted or helpless.

I'd stacked a pile of towels and an assortment of clothes in there before stepping out. I busied myself changing the bedsheets in an attempt to occupy my brain with something else other than what was going on at the moment.

It wasn't every day that a beautiful girl was showering in my apartment. But I had to admit I was more than a little apprehensive. For one thing, I didn't want her to attack me again, or to risk her using whatever magic she had to turn me into a frog or something.

I should have been more freaked out. I couldn't really believe this girl had magic at all, could I?

But instead of suspicion and mocking, the confirmation that magic and all this strangeness were, in fact, real, was coming to me as a comfort. So often I would notice blips of bizarre occurrences. Shadows that seemed to be there one second and gone the next, those 'blink and you miss it' sorts of things. Things other people would simply attribute to the randomness of the world. I'd always chalked it up to possibly my own vivid imagination, but now...

It was as if everything that previously didn't make sense in my life, suddenly and completely, now totally made sense. Like a natural revelation, something clicking into place, as opposed to the gnawing discomfort of resisting the truth for so long.

I couldn't exactly put my finger on it, but I had a gut feeling this wasn't simply someone playing a prank on me.

And despite the girl's relatively docile appearance, I knew I shouldn't underestimate her. There was no way for me to know how dangerous she was.

I really should have been more careful.

I smacked my palm on my forehead again.

Then again, how was I supposed to know that the alley I always took a shortcut through to get home from work was haunted or something?

When that freaky portal opened up, I should have run away—*run fast*. But what had I done instead? I'd stood there, gobsmacked and amazed.

Why did I have to be such a knight in shining armor anyway? I should have just left her in that alley last night.

No. I gave an immediate brisk shake of my head. I didn't think I could have ever done that.

She had been completely passed out, all alone. Even if I racked my brain again, there would have been no other option than for me to carry her all the way back to my apartment. Even if I'd been so exhausted, I'd immediately passed out too. If I'd taken her to the hospital and told the doctors how I had found her, I'd probably be sharing that padded cell with her right about now.

Besides, I could only imagine how scary it would have been—*currently must be*—for her, being in a completely different world.

Letting out a heavy sigh, I tilted my head to listen for indications she was done with the bathroom. Even if I did hate my stupid job, it paid enough. Of course, not enough for me to think nothing about wasting water.

Walking up to the door, I gave it a couple of loud knocks. "All done?"

When the door swung open (seemingly by itself), the girl was already dressed, her long pink hair damp all down her back. She was peering up at the shower head which was still streaming water—from her point of view, possibly as if from nowhere.

"The water comes from the pipes," I volunteered.

She whirled around, those violet eyes meeting mine again.

Making a face to sidestep the several puddles on the tile floor, I walked over to turn off the tap. "And the pipes get them from the city's central water store."

Her eyes narrowing, she shot me a look. "I didn't ask."

She clasped her hands together and waved one hand over her clothes.

Out of the pile I had left for her, she had chosen to wear a pair of sweats, and an old t-shirt of mine, which was peeking out at the neckline of a baggy hoodie.

I had to stop my jaw from dropping as another blurry mist covered her. When I blinked again, my clothes had somehow adjusted themselves to fit properly. The shirt and sweatpants were no longer noticeably too loose around her.

Maybe I should have dwelled on the thought of whether or not she would return my clothes to normal afterward. But again, I had to blink away that nearly overwhelming wave of disbelief that she was here for real.

Turning to me, she stuck her chin up. "I'm hungry."

Blinking blankly, my eyebrows rose. "And?"

She gave me a look as if she expected me to quickly hop like a bunny to the kitchen to prepare some kind of feast for her.

Well, of course. With her looks, she was probably a princess of some type. She probably had dozens of servants running around to do her bidding all day long.

I pursed my lips. "Look, I need to wash up first." I made a sweep of my arm to gesture her to exit the bathroom. "You can wait out there. The room is clean now." I shrugged to add, "Or, you know, find the kitchen, help yourself, make yourself at home, et cetera, et cetera."

She shot me a look that was a cross of annoyed or outraged, but also quite possibly trepidation. But again she cleared her throat, as if not wanting to seem flustered, stepped out, and slammed the door shut.

I knew I should have demanded answers from her right then. I *should* have asked her all the questions.

What kind of world was she from? What mark was she looking for on my chest before? Did she even know she'd been haunting my dreams for months? But with the tenuous nature of her presence in my world, I was half afraid that if I even breathed wrong, she would flee and disappear from my life forever.

Besides, I had to clean the mess ASAP before there was any permanent damage and I forfeited the deposit on my apartment.

With a sigh, I begrudgingly went to mopping up the floor. I threw both mine and her muddy clothes into the washing machine before hopping into the shower for a quick one. I didn't want to leave her alone for too long.

Frowning, I took a mental note that even if she could summon wind and adjust clothing, somehow, it appeared her magic wasn't able to conjure food.

Maybe there was no reason to be afraid she could turn me into a frog at all.

Either way, it was too late now. Too late to bring her back to the alley. Too late to get my head checked. I had promised her I would help her, so I would.

Besides, how bad could it be?

All I needed to do was help her find someone. I got asked for directions in the city all the time. I was pretty good at navigating, pretty good with maps. My sister always said that even if I was literally dropped into any town or city in the entire world, I could probably still manage to find my way home.

Having put on a pair of jeans from the same pile I'd left on the chair, I was drying off my hair with a towel when the distinctive sound of breaking glass grabbed my attention.

I winced. What sort of hell was she raising out there?

Dread already settling in my stomach, I strode out to the living area and screeched to a stop.

My eyes bulged. "What the—?"

4

Chapter Four - A Hazard

There was a hole in my TV.

All of the kitchen cupboards had been open and ransacked. A box of cereal lay tipped over to one side on the counter, spilling shredded wheat. A carton of eggs sat beside an open jug of milk, cracked egg shells, a glass containing three yokes—also, there was a *hole* in my TV.

The fridge door was beeping like it usually does when it's been left open for a while. At least one egg mess was splattered on the wooden floor. Several of my kitchen knives were lodged into places in the living room, the couch, part of the wall, a shelf. and through my modest flat screen—where there was a freaking *hole* in my freaking TV.

The TV screen had cracked, reflections in the black glass distorted. I wasn't entirely sure 'chef's knife through screen' could be qualified as an accident. My insurance was going to have a field day.

My mouth still dropped open, my gaze turned to the pink weirdo. She seemed breathless, her shoulders heaving, as she stood in a stance that was unmistakeable for her having just been throwing said knives.

At a complete loss, my hands fell to my sides. "Um...I see you found my knives."

For some reason, this girl thought she was well within her rights to shoot me a vehement glare. "This place is a hazard!"

Hurrying to put the milk back in the fridge before shutting the door, I couldn't help my remark, "No, *you* are a hazard. What were you even trying to do here?" I hopped around the mess on the floor so I could return all the pantry items before closing each cupboard door as I went past.

I cast a glance at the stove that was still off, relieved she hadn't accidentally set my apartment on fire. Then again, it was still early.

When I bent down to start cleaning up the egg mess, I picked up the TV remote that was lying haphazardly on the floor.

"I was told portal magic is the rarest form of sorcery. How is it that even *you* have a portal here?" Eyes still wide, she gestured toward my unluckily-slightly-out-of-warranty TV which she had destroyed. "There were intruders over there. They were trying to get into this realm. I had to stop them."

Straightening up, I closed my eyes for a moment half in exasperation, half in mirth. *Oh lord...* She must have stepped on the remote, accidentally turned the TV on, assumed the

TV show was a portal with dangerous intruders trying to sneak into this realm, and decided to defend it.

Nodding, I blew out a calming breath. "Thanks for that." I gestured for her to sit down on a bar stool at the counter. "Can you just sit there where I can see you for now—please? And *don't* move."

The look she gave me was a cross between indignation, obstinacy, but also alarm.

I put my hands up. "I promise you we're not in danger. There is no portal magic in this world. I can explain later."

Her eyes were still narrowed but she stepped over to comply.

Relief filled my chest when she didn't protest any further. Despite her overall prickliness, it was also a bit heartening to find in her that sort of vulnerability. I had to tamp down my smirk. It was threatening to feel akin to almost endearing.

Grabbing some paper towels, I went to cleaning up the mess on the floor. Good thing I kept the apartment neat and tidy for the most part. It wasn't going to take long. But after a few suspicious moments of total silence, I glanced up to see what she was doing.

Her head tilted, she was watching me clean up.

Looking down at myself, I had to pause, my face turning red. In all the rush, I didn't realize I hadn't put a shirt on yet. Swallowing hard again, I shot her a defensive look. "What?"

Her abrupt shrug was nonchalant. "I just wanted to make sure you didn't have the mark um...anywhere else."

That violet gaze was searing on my skin. Straightening up in alert, I cleared my throat. "I should finish getting dressed." A less-than-sparkling kitchen floor would have to be good enough for now. I tossed the mess into the trash and headed back to my room.

Poking my head out of the doorway so I could still keep an eye on her, I put my shirt on. "So um...this person you're looking for with this mark, what's his name?"

She didn't move from her seat, didn't turn to look at me. "I don't have his name."

I furrowed my eyebrows. "Oh okay, so you have his address?"

"No."

I blinked. "You said you had some way of locating this person?"

"I am told he is marked by a sphere of mystical convergence."

Making a face, I grabbed a hoodie before walking back to the kitchen as I pulled it on. "Then are you saying we're supposed to just walk around the city looking for this...mystical convergence what's-it?"

"Perhaps." She leveled her gaze on me. "Or if you bring me to a vantage point elevated sufficiently upon which I might scout this whole realm, it should be simple enough for me to detect which places magic has touched."

I had to blink slowly to understand her words.

It hit me like the other shoe dropping.

At the very least, I would have thought she would have some information on how to find this person. But was she seriously suggesting that I waste my day combing through the city streets in search of some hokey mystical convergence of magic?

Straining to keep my patience in check, I braced one hand on the counter. There were still cereal crumbs from the box she'd spilled. Rings of milk had congealed on the table. There was a *hole in my freaking TV.*

I was already over an hour late for work. My boss hated me enough as it was. I had to call my insurance ASAP. I still had to clean the rest of the apartment properly. I already had plans today. Not to mention Erin's party this evening where if I didn't show because I was indulging in my charitable random acts of kindness, she would no doubt torture me forever.

This was ridiculous.

Dream girl or no dream girl.

"Okay, you know what?" I pursed my lips. "I thought I could do this, but... So, look—" I ran my fingers through my hair. "I can take you to the nearest bus station or train, that's it. And then you can go look for your mystical convergence by yourself. I'm done. I've had just about enough crazy for today, thanks very much."

I moved to push her off the bar stool and veer her toward the door.

She didn't resist, which was surprising, but all the better—*wait*, what was this sharp stinging in my chest?

Wincing, I stopped short. A wispy yellow glow was forming around my hands and arms. I held up one hand. "What the hell is this?"

Glancing down, she gave me a haughty look. "That is the oath you swore."

"The what I *what*?"

"The magic manifests to remind you of your oath. It senses your resistance."

I cringed. "What does that mean exactly?"

The quirk on her lips was all kinds of self-assured. "It means if you try to abandon me or subvert me in any way, there will be...consequences. And until you fulfill your oath, you are bound to me."

"WHAT?" I groaned out loud, bracing one hand against a stool as the constriction in my chest started to spread like a million burning needles under my skin. "Oh, you have *got* to be kidding me!"

Steeling myself, I squeezed my eyes shut to breathe through what still passed for a mere slight discomfort. But I had absolutely no doubt the pain would worsen if it wore on. "Agh—are you an evil demon or something? Crap, I've just made a deal with the devil. What the hell really are you?"

Her eyes narrowed. "I am *not* a demon. Among my people, I am called a 'fae mage.'"

I clutched at my constricting throat. "Fae, like a fairy?"

Not obliging my question, her haughty gaze simply met mine again.

Ah, dammit. I should have known. She was definitely not a helpless damsel in distress. She was clever and cunning—and freaking deceitful! Of course, she'd already thought this through. She'd taken advantage of my panic and trapped me to do her bidding the first chance she saw.

This was just great. I couldn't cut her loose, couldn't leave her behind. I had no choice but to help her.

At that mere realization, the stinging in my chest eased instantly.

Oh, hell.

The fastest way to get rid of her was to complete my oath.

I threw up my hands before waving her over, sighing big and loud. "Fine. Jeez. Come on then. Let's get on with your stupid quest."

My life just turned into a videogame.

5

Chapter Five - Crossing

"These feel strange." The crazy pink con-woman/fairy I was with made a face as she gestured to the spare pair of flip-flops I'd found for her to wear.

"You're lucky Erin left them at my apartment, otherwise you'd be walking barefoot." I led down the narrow stairs of my building and out to the street. "This way." I caught her shoulder to veer back around when she turned left instead of right.

Shockingly, she didn't protest.

"You're not going to ask where we're going?" I prompted.

"I don't have to."

I scoffed in ridicule. "Oh, what, so you trust me now?"

A corner of her mouth quirked up again. "You are under oath to me. The magic will ensure you remain steadfast. It's not *you* I trust."

I rolled my eyes. *Whatever.*

The glowing on my arms had subsided, and so had the pain in my chest. And if I'd had any doubts as to the true nature of magic, they were all well and truly squashed.

A thick, hazy warmth had settled over the busy city with its usual veil of smog. Fresh asphalt, car exhaust, and the faint odor of underground prickled at my nose.

As we walked down the street, I didn't miss the several heads that turned in our direction. I totally got it though. With that fiery long hair and flawless face, she certainly wasn't the type of person who could stay below the radar.

There was a different stitch in my chest from all the guys we passed who seemed happy to openly gawk at her. She had done a little too well on whatever magic she'd applied to my old clothes. My ratty hoodie had never looked so good on anyone before.

She didn't seem to notice. Either that or she was so used to people staring that she no longer cared.

I wanted to take her arm, or put my arm around her or something, to deter any mishaps that might result in her getting so much attention.

For her protection, of course. Not for any other reason.

I gave a brisk shake of my head to refocus. "So, this person you're looking for, he's got some kind of mark on his chest, like a tattoo?"

Her response was short. "I'll know it when I see it."

"Helpful. Thanks," I mumbled wryly. "You're not going to assault him to find it like you did me, are you?"

I thought her face turned a bit red, but her tone remained even. "I didn't assault you."

"Well, maybe next time, we can simply ask."

Although, I could already see the disaster in my head. *Excuse me, sir. Would you perhaps mind taking off your shirt so we can find some sort of mystical tattoo?*

Maybe she'd figured the same thing. "If you think that will work."

Glancing up at the crossing light turning red, I moved to pull out my phone so I could text work about taking the day off while waiting on the sidewalk. Sighing, I nodded absently. "Either way, we should—" My eyes widened when she didn't stop walking. "Hey—!"

A car's long honking horn blared as it zoomed past the street. I tugged her back before she could walk further across the road, in the way of the whooshing cars of incoming traffic.

The warmth of her body was pressed against my chest. "What?" Her question was just as breathless as I felt.

"The light—you need to wait for the crossing light to turn green," I explained near her ear.

She tilted her head to give me a sideways look as if she was processing the information. "Huh." Blinking, as if snapping to attention, she pushed away more forcibly than she needed to. "You could have just said so," was her irritable response.

"You're welcome," I muttered to myself.

Shoot. That was close.

I should have been livid, annoyed, weighed down by this chore I had sworn a freaking binding oath to.

But inexplicably, what I was feeling was relief.

If I had let her set off on her little quest in the city by herself, would she even have made it to the next block?

My heart hammered in my chest at what would have happened if I hadn't been here just now.

If I wasn't here, notwithstanding all her bravado, there was no telling if she could have fallen easy prey to all sorts of dangers.

Sure, I could have maybe gotten someone else to help her out, a friend or even the police. But someone else—anyone else—may not be as careful, may not be as understanding.

Somehow—*somehow*—I was glad it was me who was here for her.

For now, she was my responsibility.

A strange stir warmed in my chest. *–the hell...?* Was I actually pleased about this?

When the crossing light finally clicked green, I grabbed her wrist to pull her along. The last thing I needed was to overthink it. "Let's go."

As I led the way to the corner diner, she tilted her chin up to look around as if she smelled something untoward. "These structures are too small to have a high vantage point of this area."

"I know," I dismissed. "Look, it's way past breakfast and I'm hungry. I'm afraid I can't go on any quests until I've had a coffee and a Bear Claw."

Her forehead creased. "A bear's claw?"

I blinked. "Oh! I mean, it's not really a bear's claw. It's just called bear—" I stopped short. "It's bread," I amended. "It's basically sweet bread with icing, a Danish pastry."

"Danish..." she repeated.

My mouth dropped open. "Uh..." I shook my head briskly. "You know what, it doesn't matter. We just have to stop in the diner for a few minutes then we can go look for your friend."

"He is not my friend."

"Or whatever." I waved to dismiss. "Go look for your mission."

The bell above the door rang when I pushed through.

Kayla's Diner was almost a city landmark.

Carl, the owner, a silver-haired man advanced in his years was behind the counter, helping a spunky teenaged girl with Pippi Longstocking braids restock the pastry cabinet. The diner was named after her, his daughter.

I also used to work here a while back, so I'd known them both for a while.

Always cheerful, Kayla already had a big smile as we walked in, but her eyes lit up when she saw who I walked in with. "Hey, Josh! So you finally got yourself a girlfriend."

I dropped the pink-haired girl's hand like it burned, my eyes bulging.

Carl chuckled good-naturedly. "Honey, you can't greet people like that." She patted her back in not-firm-at-all admonition.

I glanced down at my strange companion whose nose had wrinkled in distaste at the exchange. "Sorry," I bid before turning back to hiss pointedly at Carl and Kayla. "She's not my girlfriend."

"Oh." Kayla covered her mouth. "My bad. Sorry, Miss." She beamed a grin at me before whirling to skip back into the kitchen. "Catch you later, Josh!"

Carl rubbed his neck as he tried to recover from his daughter's faux pas, giving the girl a sheepish look. "Kayla's just kidding. These kids joke around a lot. Josh used to work for me way back when, see." Closing the cabinet, he snatched the pencil from behind his ear as he walked over. "Running late today, huh? You kids dining in? Brunch? Pancakes?"

"Uh, no, sorry. We're in a little bit of a rush. Could I just please grab a couple of Bear Claws, some coffees, and..." I cast another glance at her. "Maybe some of that special fudge?"

"Coming right up." Carl grabbed a couple of paper cups to write down our names. Looking up, he gave the girl a smile that wrinkled the corners of his eyes. "Nice to meet you, by the way. I'm Carl. What's your name?"

Her eyes narrowed in hesitation.

I pursed my lips. Oh, right. I didn't even know her name yet. How had I completely forgotten to even ask for her name all this time? Or did she not have a name? Was I supposed to make one up for her?

But then she finally spoke, "Freyjn."

"Fray..." Carl trailed off. "Eh? How do you spell that?"

I furrowed my eyebrows. I didn't know why I somehow felt that the name didn't suit her. Its sound seemed to come out of her mouth awkwardly. Then again, if she was suspicious enough of people from this world, perhaps she wasn't going to give us her real name.

"Never mind." Carl dismissed.

I craned my neck to see him write out F-R-A-Y-N.

Carl called out behind him for someone to make our coffees while he went back to grab us the pastries from the cabinet. He whistled as he worked, then he met my gaze again. "Say, Josh, did you finally find a job you're happy with?"

I made another face. "Not yet."

Chuckling, Carl looked to Freyjn to relay, "This kid has had more jobs than the weather changes. But even back when he was working for me, I could tell, he was meant for bigger things. Truth be told, I feel for him. He's so good at so many things."

I resisted the urge to roll my eyes at the exact same comment from my sister. It seemed to be the prevailing sentiment.

If only I knew what to do about it. It's not like I wanted to be aimless at this stage of my life. I just couldn't seem to find what I was passionate about. Despite everything I'd tried so far, and there had been a fair few as Carl already attested to, none of the odd jobs seemed like anything I'd want to put my heart and soul into.

So it wasn't for the lack of trying. I *still* was trying.

Carl plonked down the paper bags of pastries, sweets, and two steaming cups of coffee on the counter.

I put some bills on the tray, then reached for Freyjn's cup first to stir in sugar and cream, before lifting it to my lips to blow gently across the surface. I already knew Kayla's Diner coffees were always famously too hot.

I almost missed Carl's eyebrows raised in amusement. Stopping short, I shot him a questioning glance. "What?"

The old man stifled his chuckle. "Nothing. Absolutely nothing."

6

Chapter Six - Rules

I was pleased to see Freyjn devour the entire Bear Claw in seconds flat, and after a few awkward but curious sips of coffee, she went on to finish the drink without complaint.

She was probably still hungry. Maybe we should have sat down for a proper meal at the diner but I was sure she would have been eager to find that guy, and I certainly wanted to get all this over with as quickly as possible as well. Besides, I figured we could grab more food later.

"What are these?" She peered into the other paper bag.

"That's fudge. They're sweet," I relayed. "You'll probably like them."

She popped a piece in her mouth and slowly chewed on it.

"Carl makes them special," I added. "If there was ever a man who answered his true calling, it's Carl with food. It's good, right?" I reached for the bag to have some too, but she jumped and held it away. My jaw dropped, half in surprise, half in amusement, before I resigned. "Fine, it's all yours."

Unable to help a smile, I rubbed the back of my neck. Once Freyjn had some food in her, her countenance seemed to be less threatening, less on edge.

Her head turned to look at the stalls of fruit in front of a shop we passed along the busy street, the colorful racks of used clothing at the next shop, the dried meat cuts hung on hooks by the windows of the deli, the chattering women exiting the nail salon.

She stopped at a shop with a display of multi-colored tropical fish in medium-sized aquariums. "It's an enclosure for fish..." she mumbled.

I stuck my hands in my pockets. "People take the fish home, to keep as pets."

Her forehead creased at the notion as if it bothered her, but she merely cast her gaze up and down the busy city street, with the cars zooming past, the sunlight filtering through the elevated railroad tracks. "This is the largest market I've ever seen."

I couldn't help but watch the way those bright violet eyes widened in fascination at all the strangeness, something which I only considered normal and likely took for granted.

She stiffened at the contents of the next store—a television repair shop, where several big screens were situated behind the giant front window showing reruns of the classic TV series 'Bewitched.'

"They're not portals," I assured, tugging gently on her arm so we could walk past it. "I'll—explain later."

Her forehead was still creased. Seeming to shake it off, she merely shoved the empty paper bag at me. She'd finished all the fudge.

I grinned. *Maybe I should take her to get some ice cream.* She'd probably love that too. I knew a great milkshake place on Coney Island Avenue. I'd also once worked at a Chocolate Factory shop near that historical landmark building right on the boardwalk. Maybe Freyjn would—

Wait.

I stopped short to check myself. What on earth was I thinking? It wasn't my job to show her around the city. And this was far from a date as could be. This was some weird-ass quest. One I never asked to take on. In fact, one I was forced to take on. I couldn't wait for it to end. Right...?

Nope. Here's what I was thinking. I was thinking I wanted to stay in this oblivious little dream bubble of being with her for as long as humanly possible.

Gah.

I gave a brisk shake of my head to clear it of irrelevant thoughts—obviously stupid thoughts. Glancing up the street, I double-checked to see if the road under the bridge we needed to cross was no longer under construction.

Not too far to go.

When we came to another street crossing, I was relieved when Freyjn noted the red light and stopped by herself. When the light turned green, she took my lead and walked across with me.

Mrs. Buchman and her dog were coming down the path toward us on their daily walk, a routine they must have been doing for years. At one point, I had a job walking dogs and hers was one so I raised my hand in a wave, "Good morning, Ma'am."

"Hello, young man." There was a hitch in her smile when she noticed I wasn't alone. Her eyebrow rose as if in delight, but before she could muse aloud the same thing as Kayla, I quickened my pace.

"Enjoy your day!" I bid with a mock salute, even as I kept one eye on Freyjn to make sure she was still following me.

I almost shook my head in disbelief again. Was it so unusual for me to be walking around with a pretty girl? Racking my brain, I supposed I couldn't actually recall the last time I'd gone on a date that wasn't a simple hour-long confinement in a fancy restaurant.

Also—again, this wasn't a date.

But Freyjn was watching them walk away with narrowed eyes.

"Are you thinking that little dog sort of looked like that lady?"

The blink of surprise on Freyjn's face told me I guessed correctly.

I stifled my laughter. "It happens."

At the next corner, one of the regular unhoused people was situated with his shopping cart of treasures.

Pausing for a second, I fished out some coins from my pocket. "Hey, Rufus." I greeted with a nod, dropping my coins into his hat on the floor.

"Thank you kindly," he replied with a feigned tip of an invisible hat.

Freyjn's eyes were narrowed again as we kept walking. She craned her neck back for a moment as the man eased back against the stoop of the building doorway, before prompting me, "Do you know everyone in this realm?"

"Oh. No, I don't know everyone." I paused to think. "I mean, I suppose I do know a lot of people in this area. I've worked all over the place and see the same people every day. This is just—it's my neighborhood and I think it's good to be friendly. You probably have the same sort of things in your world, right? Right...?" I trailed off my rambling.

She shot me another odd look but said nothing.

Or...maybe not. Okay, shut up, Josh.

When we reached the boardwalk, Freyjn's gaze roved around once again in complete fascination. Her violet eyes glittered as she took in the fine, blue skies which made the water sparkle bright along the beach. The seagulls flew overhead. The distinctive salty air mingled with the fresh breeze.

Was it possible Freyjn was even enjoying herself?

There was a stir in my stomach of almost eagerness. Maybe it *wouldn't* be such a bad idea if I showed her around more of the city...

Ah, Josh. Get a grip.

Dumb quest. *Not* a date. Potentially vengeful fairy who might blast me to kingdom come whenever her glucose levels were low.

Looking away, I ran my fingers through my hair again. "Um, hey, let me know if you're still hungry. There's a guy with a hotdog cart nearby who owes me a favor."

When she didn't respond, I glanced back.

Freyjn had paused a few feet back on the boardwalk. She seemed mesmerized by the guy with a makeshift cardboard table doing the shell game by the park fence.

"*Watch closely, watch very closely—*" the guy was droning on to the small crowd that had gathered around him.

Oh dear lord.

One of the magicians was doing an 'escape artist' bit and making a show of getting out of being all bound in thick ropes inside a sack on the ground.

I made a face. Any boy scout who knew his knots could do the same thing. When I was younger, I often did similar tricks for our family at parties.

Groaning inwardly again, I trudged back to grab her wrist. "Let's go."

"But I've already figured out the trick," Freyjn started as I led her away. "It's really easy."

"No, it's not. Come on."

We passed a couple more street magicians—I mean, this was Brooklyn, and people had to make a living somehow.

Freyjn tugged her arm back. "Oh, but look, that is the simplest form of magic." She gestured to one guy making objects appear to float in mid-air. "Is it normal in this realm to perform enchantments on such a casual occasion as this?"

Without waiting for my response, she clasped her hands together.

It was a good thing I hadn't taken my eyes off her at all, since her entire body began to emanate a smoky purple glow, and there was that wind again which seemed to come from nowhere, teasing at her wild hair.

Jumping in alert, I grabbed both her hands. "Whoa, hey!"

"Ow—!" The wind and the purple smoke dissipated instantly.

I cast furtive glances everywhere to make sure nobody saw, but luckily everyone else was distracted by the other street performers.

I hissed my warning, "You shouldn't be doing that magic stuff around other people."

Her annoyed gaze up at me was beginning to feel very familiar. "Why?"

"Well, in this world—this realm, we actually don't have magic. Not for real anyway. Those guys, they just do tricks and illusions." I shook my head pointedly. "If they see you doing your real magic, you might freak people out and they'll call the cops. And well, I'm pretty sure they won't be as understanding as I am, alright?"

Her head was tilted to one side as she considered my words.

I wasn't sure I had time to explain all the nuances of this world to Freyjn, but I was going to have to start somewhere.

I rubbed my face with one hand. "Maybe we should have gone through some rules before we left my apartment—okay, look. Rule number 1: No magic in public. Rule number 2: You have to stay with me. You can't be wandering off. I don't know how things work in your world, but this world is dangerous."

Her eyebrows snapped together as if in ridicule. "I have powers you cannot even fathom. I can take care of myself."

"It's not that," I assured. "It's just...there are some things that—*ugh*." How on earth could I possibly explain? I tried again, "This is Brooklyn, see? You'll want to stay away from strangers. Just-just trust me on this, alright? I'm the only one who can keep you safe."

Her eyes lit up in surprise when I said that word.

I belatedly realized that when I'd stopped her doing magic, I had actually pulled her against me, her hands still held in my grip.

For a split second, I was overcome with another strange sensation—a fleeting ripple of a hazy recollection, as if this moment in time folded in on itself, familiar details surfacing from nowhere...

I had a sudden urge to lift my hand and tuck her hair back behind her ear.

Freyjn's wide eyes snapped back up to meet mine. She pulled away in alarm and averted her gaze altogether.

I blinked, snapping back to reality. Shoot, what were we talking about again? "Um." I cleared my throat as it all came back to me. "Look, just—just promise me, you won't do magic in front of other people, okay?" I instructed as firmly as I could without sounding threatening.

Her eyes narrowed again. "Are you asking me to swear an oath to you as well?"

I stopped short to correct. "N-No. Not an oath. Just...just a promise."

Freyjn neither acknowledged nor protested.

I blew out a sigh. I had been wrong earlier. It was in everyone's interest to conclude this quest as soon as possible.

Even if I dared to admit that I enjoyed her company, it wasn't safe for her to stay here any longer than was required.

I beckoned her over. "We'd better keep moving."

"Tell me we aren't actually walking aimlessly around this realm."

"Of course not. You said you needed to find a high vantage point," I repeated. "Well, I had an idea." We walked up the street some more and I gestured upward. "You're not afraid of heights, are you?"

7

Chapter Seven - Heights

From the street, Luna Park burst into view as a kaleido-scope of color, its towering rides and large signs loom-ing against the bright skyline. The iconic roller coaster sat silently on its track, while the spokes of the Ferris wheel and its unmoving carriages merely glinted in the sunlight.

The park only opened at noon, so the usual riotous laugh-ter, music, and merrymaking hadn't yet overtaken the dis-tant crashing of waves blending with the hum of the city.

I checked my watch. "The place is still closed for another half hour or so but my buddy Artie works here. I might be able to ask a favor."

As we approached one of the smaller gates, Freyjn was rubbernecking around in curiosity again. "Did you used to work here before as well?"

I shrugged. "I've worked in a lot of places." Pulling out my phone, I frowned at the several unread messages waiting and a couple of missed calls. *Ah, crap.* I'd actually forgotten to notify work that I wouldn't be in today.

Shaking my head, I sent out a short message to my boss—one he likely wouldn't be happy with either way, before shooting a quick call to Artie to let him know I was here.

Artie worked the ticket booth at Luna Park so it didn't take him long to meet us at the side entrance. Burly with buzz-cut blond hair, we were about the same age. "Hey, Josh!" Letting us through the door, he gave me a high-five before his gaze easily turned to Freyjn. "Wow, you finally got a girlfriend?"

I almost groaned out loud again. "She's *not* my girlfriend. Why is everyone asking me this?" I threw up my hands in disbelief, before gesturing to one and then the other. "Freyjn, this is my friend Artie. Artie, this is Freyjn." I gave Artie a pointed look. "I'm just helping her find someone, okay?"

Artie's laughter was booming and boisterous. "My bad. Sorry, man."

I rolled my eyes. "Could you just do me a favor and let us up the Ferris wheel? There's a..." I stopped short, cringing. "Um, it's a bit hard to explain."

Artie thumped on my back. "Say no more, my friend. I know some girls like freaky stuff."

I shot Freyjn an indignant, sheepish look, before hissing at Artie, "It's not like that!"

He burst out laughing all over again. "Whatever, man."

Sighing, I knew there was no point arguing with him, and the faster I acquiesced, the less trouble he was going to give me. "We just need maybe ten, fifteen minutes, tops," I assured, giving him a fist bump. "I'll owe you, dude."

Artie led us to the Ferris wheel ride and opened the gate so we could walk onto the platform. He unlatched the carriage door for us, and I let Freyjn step in first before Artie shut it behind us.

"Thanks, pal."

Moving to sit across the bench from Freyjn, I gave her an apologetic look. "Hey, look, I'm so sorry about Artie. Sometimes his brain disconnects from his big mouth."

Freyjn's forehead was still creased with a frown—perpetually, it seemed. "It's a bit odd that these people see it fit to pry about your calliances. Do you often parade your many *girlfriends* in front of them?"

Indignant protest surged in my chest. "No! I swear I don't even have girlfriends. Not for a super long time. You're the first girl I've ever—um," I flustered. "I mean, it's probably because you're the first girl they've ever seen out with me." I shook my head. "Just—please, don't mind it. They're only curious about you. They're really nice people otherwise. Really."

She merely quirked an eyebrow as if she didn't even care about my (admittedly, too lengthy) explanation. She jerked in her seat when the carriage shifted as the Ferris wheel started to move. "What...what's going on?"

Glancing out the window, I caught Artie's casual wave up at us from his position behind the machinery booth.

Freyjn's eyes widened as the distance between us and the ground grew. I thought she would be freaked out but the more our Ferris wheel carriage went up, the more excited she looked.

"This is...amazing." Her mouth hung open as she gazed out the window. "How high can we go on this? It's as if we are climbing to the sky."

I pursed my lips. "Not quite that high."

Once the carriage had stopped right at the very top, I gestured out the window, almost pleased with myself. "There you go. A high enough vantage point of this area. Knock yourself out."

Freyjn turned eagerly out the window, short of pressing her nose against the glass.

With a low chuckle, I braced my hands against my window frame.

I could almost see clear through to the western bridge. Streams of people hurried up and down the boardwalk. Behind us, the street was lined with tall apartment buildings. Across the other way, along the rest of the waterfront where the sandy beaches ended, transitioned into the next neighborhood.

Freyjn's eyes were narrowed in concentration. "There. I see something. It's a haze of magic swirling around east of here." She tilted her head, her gaze unfocused. "And I'm...sensing a sort of chill, a cold but stagnant breeze. It feels like it is near a type of inlet of water."

Even as I squinted, I didn't have the slightest clue what she thought she could be seeing or feeling over there. "Inlet of water?" I moved a bit closer since I would have to have an idea where she was intending to go if I was supposed to take her there. All I could see was the tops of trees, roofs of low-rise buildings. "What does it mean?"

"It means something magical has made its home over there. That's where we need to go."

Still frowning, I took out my phone to load an online map. There was no way I was going to simply eyeball this. I shifted my gaze up to the horizon and down at my phone a few times, spinning the map around, trying to make my best guess estimate where exactly we needed to go. Perhaps the docks along the bay...?

"What are you doing?"

"Looking at a map."

"On that?" Her forehead creased. "Did you not use that device to communicate with your friend before?"

"Yeah." I nodded. "It does that too. It does a lot of things, like..." I paused for a moment, before lifting my phone to hold it far away enough to take a selfie. "This."

Except somehow, the flash was on and the bright light popped in our faces.

With a stifled scream, Freyjn jumped in shock. She stumbled to the floor. The next thing I knew, the entire Ferris wheel carriage was covered in a thick layer of frost.

"What the hell—?" I braced myself back against the frigid cold metal bench opposite her—but recoiled quickly as the arctic metal about near burned my fingertips. *Holy crap!* I could see my breath in the air. The temperature around us had dropped significantly. Icicles had formed in the corners of the carriage roof above us.

Trying not to visibly shiver, I helped her up. "Oh my god, are you okay?"

"What the hell did you do that for?" she cried out.

"Me? What the hell did *you* do that for?" I retorted.

Craning my neck to look out the window, I was relieved to find that we were likely too high up for Artie to see that our carriage was a giant block of ice. Also hoping that we didn't plummet to our deaths if the ice somehow caused the carriage to break off from the wheel altogether.

Luckily, the ice was already melting from the seasonal warm weather.

Rubbing my face in relief, I sank back against the seat again. Remorse squeezed my chest when I met her livid gaze again. "I'm sorry. I didn't mean to scare you. It was just a camera."

"A what?"

"Never mind. I'll explain later."

My brain was already exhausted. The list of things I was going to need to explain to her later was growing by the minute.

Still miffed, Freyjn pursed her lips. "Did your little device of death at least tell you where we need to go then?"

I rolled my eyes first. "Yes. Looks like it's in the next neighborhood, near the docks."

She shifted in her seat. I wanted to be mad. Again, I really wanted to be. But I could tell she was really startled by the camera flash. And even if the frown on her face indicated upset, I could also tell how disoriented she was.

Having to pretend to be strong on the outside was something I definitely had first-hand experience with as well.

When I met her gaze again, mine was tempered with sympathy. "It's okay." I cracked a grin to reassure her. "That was...pretty cool."

Freyjn's frown collapsed into a look of mock ridicule.

"It's a pun—"

"Yeah, I got that," she snapped in pointed exasperation.

Averting my gaze for a moment, I couldn't stop the stupid grin spreading on my face. But when I turned to her again, I almost caught my breath.

She wasn't looking at me, but those violet eyes were sparkling, the corners of her mouth turned up, her shoulders almost shaking in mirth.

My heart pounding in my chest, my spirits soared. I just made her laugh. She was actually smiling...because of me.

I almost blinked in a startle when the carriage jerked again to begin its movement back down.

Oh, of course. I noted with dejection. Just when I was starting to make headway with her. I supposed I shouldn't have been expecting to catch any breaks.

8

Chapter Eight - Camouflage

As we left the Ferris wheel, I shook Artie's hand in appreciation before hurrying to catch up with Freyjn. The rude little fairy had sauntered off with not even a word of thanks.

See, I wanted to think that. That she was nothing but a rude, little, presumptuous magical being.

That moment that had passed between us, shorter than fleeting though it may have been, was quickly replaced by urgency.

I wasn't even sure why I could seem to read her so well.

And was this really a simple errand as she had initially indicated? Was anything she'd told me so far true at all?

Except...

It was shocking how much it actually didn't matter to me.

Shocking how much I didn't care about the details.

This girl... I watched Freyjn walk along the path ahead of me.

Her wild hair bright even against the backdrop of the empty amusement park with colorful rides and game booths, she glanced over her shoulder to meet my gaze for a moment.

I clenched my jaw in full certainty, in the deepest of convictions.

I would do anything for this girl...

Handfuls of people were beginning to stream into the park with their merry chattering din. I check my watch for the time. The park had already opened.

Freyjn's eyes narrowed as she noted the same thing. "We must move on quickly."

"Agreed." I moved to take her arm so we could leave.

Her manner had reverted to wary, tense. I wondered if she was hungry again. "Say, you never mentioned if you're against some sort of deadline. Like, do we need to find this mystical convergence before midnight or you turn into a pumpkin?"

"I need to—" Her urgent rant stopped short. She wrinkled her nose to echo in ridicule, "Pumpkin?"

I blinked. "Oh. It's a fairy tale about a princess—you know what, never mind." I waved to dismiss. "I was just making a joke."

She almost scoffed. "How can you make jokes at a time like this?"

I shrugged. "I don't know. I guess it's what I do when I'm nervous." I put my hands up. "Not that I'm nervous to be with you—" I winced. "Not *with* you, just...around you. The situation—" I added to correct. "I mean, I'm nervous about the situation. Like in case there's like danger or something. Like harmful, physical danger—*not physical*, I mean, not in that way." I cringed. Crap. Why couldn't I shut up? "I mean, dying—like, you know? You know what I mean, right—right?" I bit my lip to stop babbling.

She glared at me in irritable disbelief.

I cleared my throat. "So *are* we in danger? Besides from people from innocent televisions trying to come into this world?" I joked again—thought I was joking. I really should stop.

As we passed the funnel cake stand, her walking slowed.

I furrowed my eyebrows at the dread on her face. "What's wrong?"

Her head was tilted to one side as if she was straining to hear the faintest noise.

Did she have something like a Spidey sense? *Was* she sensing danger?

I cast a glance around us. A mother was laughing fondly at her toddler eagerly getting into his freshly spun cotton candy. A group of teenagers wearing party hats were running toward their first ride with loud excited shouts, a pair of grandparents had immediately found a bench to retire on.

I marveled at the small group of men who walked past the guy setting up to sell balloons. "Oh wow, those guys are really into cosplay."

Clad in dark, uniform leather reinforced with polished blackened steel plates and matching gauntlets, shiny spears clanking metal against metal, the group sauntered down the path.

Freyjn's tone turned ominous. "I thought I had more time before they tracked me."

"Who? Those guys wearing costumes?"

Her expression grim, she pulled me back behind the popcorn booth. "Those are not costumes."

I teetered on my stance to regain my balance.

Not costumes…?

Cold dread crept into my insides.

Oh, shoot. I swallowed hard as I almost caught the eye of one of them. I walked further behind the row of game booths, pulling Freyjn along, trying to duck my head low.

"Oh boy, this is going to get really interesting, really fast." I assessed the growing crowd of families and children with concern, but the park-goers didn't seem at all startled by the horde of menacing armed warriors barging through the thick of them.

Before I could wonder about the crowd's non-reaction, the horde walked past a line of fun house mirrors. "Whoa." I glanced from the reflections in the mirror back to the horde. As far as anyone else would have been concerned, they were only a group of big bullies wearing letter jackets, instead of leather and armor and pointy weapons.

I blinked a few times to make sure I wasn't seeing things. "H-how are they doing that?"

"It's a glamor." Freyjn quickly pulled her hoodie on to cover her bright hair as we sneaked past a big tour group. "My people can use it to fool those from this realm into seeing something else. It's similar to what I've done to these clothes." She gestured down at herself.

"How come I can see what they really are?"

She shrugged. "It's likely because of the oath you've sworn to me. Some of my magic has extended to you, to protect you from this very thing." Unfortunately, when she glanced up next, that's when the horde spotted us.

"Look! Over there!" A yell punctuated the din as the fiends began to push and shove toward our direction.

"Uh-oh." Jumping in alert, I grabbed Freyjn's arm again so we could take off running. Not before something whizzed past my head—a bullet? An arrow? I didn't even want to ask.

Ducking lower, I cursed out loud. "Holy crap! Are they shooting at us?"

"We need to lead them away from all these innocent people," Freyjn called out.

Picking up our pace, I led Freyjn down the narrow path behind the snack stands and toward the isolated far edge of the amusement park, behind a roller coaster under maintenance.

My breathing was turning ragged. "How the heck did these guys even get here?"

Creeping up beside me, she gave me an even look. "Do you really have to ask? They are warriors from a superior realm. They can go wherever they please."

There was a sting of offense in my chest, but I decided to let the 'superior' realm comment slide due to the obviously more pressing matters at hand.

We slipped behind an empty ticket booth, squeezing into a gap littered with spent tickets and confetti.

Voices grew louder as the warriors approached. Coming around the corner, two of them stalked past our hiding spot, their massive spears looked absolutely nothing like movie props.

My heart pounded in my chest. This day was getting better and better. My frayed thoughts went into a tailspin.

Was this how it ends? Today? On a mundane Thursday afternoon.

I still had nothing to show for my perfectly average life. I hadn't achieved anything yet nor made a name for myself. Cold sweat threatened to trickle down my neck at the sense of inescapable peril.

On the other hand, Freyjn's eyebrows were furrowed in resolve, fists clenched tight. All of the anxiety, vulnerability, and disorientation that seemed to overwhelm her before was gone. Her violet eyes were sharp, focused—and it hit me.

This. This was her wheelhouse.

She wasn't a princess.

She was a warrior.

As if to prove my point, Freyjn cursed under her breath. "I couldn't bring my daggers to this realm. Can you use a sword? Do you know how to fight?"

My eyes widened. "What? I mean, I can throw a mean punch, but there's no way I'm any match for those guys!" I shot her a look, my question hushed, "Can't your magic deal with them?"

Her forehead creased. "I thought you told me not to use magic."

I gestured around us. "There's no one else here to see. Besides, that wasn't an oath. I mean, a promise is sort of the same—" I stopped to dismiss. "Never mind."

Hesitating, she pursed her lips. "My magic has limitations in this realm. I can only do certain things or I might exhaust it."

"Couldn't we just talk to them? Maybe we can work something out?" I ventured.

The look she gave me was a cross between disbelief and ridicule.

"Okay, no." I shrugged, cringing again.

Shooting another glance out, I blew out a sigh of relief when the two warriors had moved on.

Pulling on Freyjn's hand, I led the way to creep back out from the rear of the ticket booth, so we could make a mad dash toward the park's exit through an alley behind some fake building structures.

But as we came around a corner, two hulking warriors appeared to block our path. Their weapons drawn, faces dark as they closed in.

Skidding to a stop, I swallowed past the dry lump in my throat.

We were trapped.

9

Chapter Nine - Mirrors

Before I could rack my brain for what to do next, Freyjn shoved me back behind her.

Her frown deepening in determination, she clasped her hands together before doing some type of *Tai chi* move.

Bright light seared my eyes. I squeezed them shut.

When I opened them again, the two warriors were sprawled on the floor, unconscious.

My jaw dropped. "Whoa! What did you just do?"

The usual purple smoke and inexplicable wind swirling around Freyjn was already dissipating.

She let out a breath, steadying herself in her stance. "I struck them with a force of wind."

I was still gobsmacked. "You can do that?"

"I can use my elemental magic to generate sharp bursts of—" She briskly shook her head. "You know what, never mind. I'll explain later."

"There's more of them." I tapped repeatedly on her arm as my eye caught six or seven of them split into two groups just past the ticket booth.

"Too many." Freyjn gritted her teeth. "I'll lead them away. You go hide in one of those sheds."

Jarred by her statement, I blinked. "I'm not leaving you."

Shaking her head, she moved to step out to the path. "I'll deal with them. I can take care of myself."

Frowning, I caught her arm. "Shut up. I'm not leaving you."

Her glare was indignant, but she must have noted the determined set of my chin. I wasn't going to budge. Sighing, she dropped her protest. "Well, how do you suppose you're going to fight them? You're just a regular weak human boy."

I shot her another mocking look. "Hey, not everything has to be solved with violence." Racking my brain, I cast a glance around us and an idea struck me almost instantly. "We need to run into that." I pointed across the path toward the huge 'Haunted Mirror Maze' attraction with the 'under construction' sign.

Freyjn's eyes narrowed but she nodded after a mere second. "Go. I'll cover."

Tugging her along with me, I shot out of our hiding place to duck in through the side of the fake haunted house, squinting amidst the bright sparks of light popping all around us. I assumed Freyjn was deflecting whatever those warriors were shooting at us.

I didn't have time to glance back. As soon as I'd closed the door and the darkness of the house swallowed us, I led

Freyjn through the tricky maze, along a path I already knew like the back of my hand. Passing a fake zombie, I grabbed the costumed mannequin to drag along.

Then stopping at a relatively spacious juncture in the maze, I rummaged through a fake treasure chest for more costumes and props.

The door to the maze crashed open. Rumbling footsteps thundered against the wooden floor panels as the warriors attempted to make their way through.

Freyjn's grip on my arm tightened. "They're here."

I wasn't worried. If the warriors had even bothered with the glamor for their appearance, they likely wouldn't want to use magic to blast through the entire maze and call undue attention to themselves. There was no way they would be able to navigate through the unfamiliar darkness to find us.

Stopping near the wall, I flicked a few switches in the control board behind a panel which turned on the music, a bit of fake rattling, creaky footsteps, and howling to disguise our movements

I'd taken us to a very specific spot in the maze. A hidden space intended to mislead others into thinking they knew where you were. It was nearly inaccessible except to park staff.

The warriors would be able to see 'us' (or the dummies I was setting up), but it would take them a while to reach us, or to even figure out they'd been deceived.

Once I'd set up the decoys, I tugged on Freyjn's arm once again. "This way."

I led her toward a hidden corner and bent down to open a wooden trap door on the floor. Crouching low beneath the floorboards, I crept on in the relative darkness.

The heavy footfalls of the warriors thumped close above our heads—too close.

Mildew and thick dust stifled my breathing. My heart pounded in my chest. I was half afraid they would somehow catch our scent and then stomp right through the wooden floor to grab us. But their steps seemed to be going around the route of the mirror maze, around and around, but no further.

Gritting my teeth in determination, I didn't stop moving until we had traveled through the connecting building structures, to emerge out of a matching trap door clear across the park.

When we popped out from beneath the wooden floorboards, I took in a deep breath of the fresh salty air, then glanced back to note that we were no longer being pursued—at least, for the moment.

Whew. It actually worked.

Of course, I could probably never use that trick on them again.

Relieved, I sagged against a wall by the gift shop buildings to catch my breath. I looked at Freyjn again, almost in an expectant prompt. *How's that for a regular weak human boy?*

Having grasped what I'd done, she merely rolled her eyes. "We should get out of here," she declared, moving past me to walk on ahead.

Shaking my head, I figured I really shouldn't expect much gratitude from her.

Jumping to catch up with her, I led the way out to another side exit only used by the park staff, and once we got out to the street, we made a break for it.

"We need to find someplace to hide until they regroup," Freyjn noted. "Somewhere dark. With a lot of people."

I nodded. "I know just the place."

We raced down the road toward the boardwalk, dodging the mid-afternoon crowds milling around a car park.

I cast her a curious glance. "So who *were* those guys chasing us?"

Her face darkened. "I told you, they are warriors from my realm. They mean to take me back and I am certain they will use any means necessary to do so." Her jaw clenched again. "But I can't go back yet. Not without completing my mission."

"What the hell?" My eyes bulged. "Are you saying there's magical soldiers coming after us and trying to capture us now? You didn't mention that when I swore that oath to help you."

"You didn't ask." She shrugged. "For future reference, I would advise that before you swear any more oaths, you really ought to get all the details."

Groaning, I smacked my palm to my forehead. "Gee, thanks."

Freyjn's eyes caught the 'No entry' symbol on the signage plastered on the side door to the building I'd swung open for her, almost hidden in the foliage. "Let me guess. You used to work here before too?"

I shrugged. "Just for one summer."

Through a few more doors, up and down a few staircases, I finally stopped in a dimly lit room behind a large tank of blue water.

The other side of the tank was the main exhibit area of the New York Aquarium.

A handful of children and their parents were marveling up at the hundreds of marine species swimming about beyond the thousand-foot-wide glass wall. Although, the noise of the crowd was muted from all the way back here.

Breathless, I braced my hands on my knees. "We should be safe enough now."

Overhead, the aquarium played ambient sounds of being underwater, sort of echoey, hollow, almost eerie. Ethereal blue bathed the darkened space, wavy sparkles of light shone in different patterns across the walls and the floors.

Freyjn's mouth had dropped open as she assessed the sheer size of the glass tank with all kinds of sea life swimming about. "This is..."

I grinned. "Incredible, isn't it?"

Blinking slowly, she ran her hands up and down her arms like she was cold. "Sad," she finished with a word I wasn't expecting.

"Sad?" I echoed in question.

Stepping up to the glass, she pressed one hand flat against it. "Do these creatures know they are merely circling in this enclosed world? Unable to roam free in the vast ocean?"

I pointed to one of the larger creatures seemingly gliding in the water. "Well, see, that there's a shark. People would rather watch them from a safe distance like this, because they are usually thought of as dangerous."

She turned to me. "But are they?"

I considered the look on her face. "Good question." I was less interested in shark facts than I was about why Freyjn seemed preoccupied with the notion of enclosures, much like she had noted with the fish at the pet shop on the street.

I pursed my lips in concern. "Do you want to go somewhere else?"

She shook her head.

"Are you sure we're safe here?"

"My presence should be masked by all these humans. They shouldn't find me again too fast." She sighed. "Minor charms and a bit of glamor should have been safe enough to stay undetected, but I fear those warriors must have sensed my ice magic when I accidentally used it at that giant wheel."

I cringed. That was my fault. "Sorry."

Her forehead was still creased, but she merely stepped back, clutching at her stomach.

Hungry.

"Oh!" My eyes lit up. I gestured toward the green glow of the vending machine right around the corner. "I'll get us some food."

10

Chapter Ten - Safe

I nearly cleaned out the vending machine of its snacks. I wasn't sure what she liked, so I'd gotten *everything*. A rolled-up canvas sign I found from a nearby table thrown across the floor served as a makeshift picnic blanket.

Freyjn took her time and worked her way through several sandwiches, mini tubs of yogurt, pudding, fresh fruit cups, and cookies.

I cracked a smirk. I supposed being chased by other-worldly warriors around the city would make anyone starving.

Checking my watch, I sighed half in relief. It seemed our hiding place was an effective one. We'd been here a good hour with no further imminent threat from the bad guys. I imagined by this time, those brutes should be giving up soon, if not already.

Propping my knee up, I leaned against the back wall to tear open the small crinkly bag in my hands.

Freyjn looked over. "What is that?"

"Oh. Fish crackers, you want some?"

"Did you say...fish crackers?"

I nodded. "Uh-huh." I plucked another bag from the pile of food on our mat and held it out for her. "Here. Try one."

She seemed to marvel at the little packet in her hand. "This is food?" She lifted the item to her mouth to try to bite into it.

Putting my hand up to stop her, I almost laughed. "Oh, you need to open the bag first. Here, let me."

Freyjn stared at my hands as I tore open the package. Her eyes were narrowed again.

As if she was thinking hard about something... as if she was straining to remember...

I gave her back the packet. "What is it?"

She just gave a brisk shake of her head. "Nothing."

Tilting her head as she chewed, she gazed up at the big blue tank, her eyes roving around to survey our surroundings. "Is nobody going to mind that you're hiding out back here?" She noted the breadcrumbs, plastic containers, and empty packets already strewn across the floor. "Or that we're making a big mess?"

I shrugged. "It's an emergency. I'm sure the aquarium head honcho, Owen, would understand. Besides, I've seen bigger messes than this. Certainly do a lot of cleaning up other people's messes at my current job. I mean, I don't like it, but..." I trailed off with a grimace.

Freyjn noted the potential ire leaking into my words. "Is that why everyone's been saying you hate your job?"

Still cringing, I scratched my head. "I guess... I really think my boss Andrew assigned me this post out of spite. Plus, I feel he has sort of a selective vision when it comes to his workers." I sank against the wall as I relayed my story. "Like this guy, Ron at work can never seem to do anything wrong. He'll miss meetings and deadlines, sure, but does he ever get told off? Nope. Meanwhile, here I am doing the work of three people—fielding quite a few complaints about Ron, by the way, and all Andrew will see, is that somehow I *missed* something."

Her eyebrows knitted together. "That makes absolutely no sense."

An easy reminder that the real world still exists, my shoulders tensed at the notion of going back to work tomorrow to have to explain my absence today to Andrew.

A bit dejected, I picked at the frayed knees of my jeans. "It's funny. People say I'm good at a lot of things. But I never seem to measure up to whatever imaginary lofty standard Andrew's set. Which is weird because he's far from perfect himself. In fact, he can be quite a jerk. He once told one of my colleagues, she couldn't go home to deal with an emergency with her son, like—"

Too annoyed at the recall, I couldn't even finish. I merely rubbed my face. "Either way, he just gives all of us so much grief. If people had a choice, I'm sure they would look for work elsewhere in a heartbeat."

Freyjn crunched through her words. "You ought to tell him off."

I sucked a breath between my teeth. "Well, see, I can't really do that. He's my boss, and technically, I should be following his orders."

"Is he a king?" Her prompt was haughty. "Surely, he cannot have final say over everything."

I gave a resigned shrug. "Well, he does in my company. Here in this world, he's called the CEO though, not king. But I suppose that's close enough."

She let out a thoughtful sigh. "I can um...relate. There is also someone I know who can be quite particular. She also insists on having everything perfect. It's as if there is no place for anything else in the world."

I was pleasantly surprised she felt comfortable enough to share. Also somewhat fascinated that she sort of understood where I was coming from. I elbowed her. "See? You understand."

Freyjn gave me a soft smile that almost took my breath away.

In the dim light, the coloring of her hair looked neon as she held my gaze.

I wanted time to stop.

I couldn't help the stray thought that I would be perfectly content to sit beside her on the floor behind this giant aquarium if I could look into her eyes all day long.

For the hundredth time today, I felt an overwhelming wave of bewilderment. I still couldn't believe the beautiful girl from my dreams was actually here with me, smiling at me.

Then I realized I probably shouldn't be staring at her for so long.

Except, Freyjn was also studying my face. Those sparkling eyes burned into me—curious, analyzing, incredulous, but at the same time...relieved, relaxed.

Safe.

I blinked slowly. I didn't know how I knew how she felt, but I did.

Right then, with me...Freyjn felt safe.

Almost tentatively, I reached over to brush off cookie crumbs from one corner of her mouth. "You've got some..." My fingers brushing against that soft cheek, there was a fresh twinge in my chest. Though I was fairly certain the magic oath wasn't the reason I couldn't breathe at the moment...

Before my gaze could even dare drop to her lips, I jerked to straighten up in my seat, clearing my throat.

Freyjn winced at my unexpected gesture, but she quickly averted her own gaze in discomfort.

I noted her slight movement, shifting *away* from me on the mat. I looked away myself. "Um, do you think the coast should be clear now?"

That puzzled furrow on her brows came back. "The coast is...outside."

"I mean—" I stopped short but waved my hand in the air. "Never mind. We can probably go now." I collected all the trash to throw away, restored the canvas sign, then beckoned her to follow me once again.

Our little hidden nook must have been a signal dead zone inside the aquarium building. As soon as we exited the structure, my phone started buzzing crazily in my pocket. Taking it out to look, my eyes bulged. "Whoa."

Seventeen missed calls.

Crap.

Some were from work. Some were from—

I checked the time. "Oh shoot, I almost forgot about Erin's birthday party tonight." I glanced up and down the busy city block, where the lengthening shadows of late afternoon fell across the streets before my gaze landed on Freyjn again.

She gave me a prompting look. "What?"

"I think I have to take you to my sister's birthday party."

"What?" Freyjn's expression turned mocking. "This is not a time to be attending festivities. We must get to the docks immediately. I must complete my mission."

I pursed my lips in resolve. "Well, tough. Since it's clearly too risky for you to be gallivanting around the island by yourself, I'm going to have to put that oath on hold—until after my sister's party."

Pausing to verify that I could still breathe, I checked my limbs in satisfaction as the restrictive glowing of the oath magic had not manifested. "And it seems the oath agrees with me. I'm not subverting you. I'm just...delaying for a bit."

Freyjn's lips curled in distaste.

"Besides, there'll be tons of humans at the party," I rationalized further. "You should be masked pretty well."

She was still glaring at me.

"Plus, there's going to be lots of food there."

Her eyes lit up in an instant.

I almost laughed but decided not to point it out. I gave Freyjn's clothes an assessing look before looking down at myself as well. "We'll need to go back to my apartment to get changed first."

11

Chapter Eleven - My Friend

I was a bundle of nerves walking with Freyjn to the party.

The last traces of sunlight were fading into deep indigo as the night prepared to take over the sky.

Erin's boyfriend's apartment was only a few blocks away from mine, but Freyn was attracting so much attention from passers-by that I had to severely tamp down the urge to growl.

Again, not that I could blame them.

I'd just pulled on a pair of stonewashed jeans straight from the dryer and a black leather jacket I rarely got use out of.

But when Freyjn had stepped out of my bedroom after getting changed. my heart almost stopped. I hadn't even realized I'd stood up from the couch.

Her long hair was fixed into a loose braid down her back. Her cheeks tinted pink, those violet eyes sparkling. She was wearing that dress she'd come through to this world with. I didn't know what that fabric was called, but it complimented every curve of her figure. She shimmered with all the colors of the rainbow.

She was...absolutely stunning.

Absolutely perfect.

She'd frowned again at my stare.

All I could babble on about was my relief that the washing machine didn't ruin the fabric of her dress, since it didn't have any care instructions, if it was hand-wash only, or dry clean, or no tumble dry...

Nope, I just couldn't stop being awkward.

I seriously wanted to kick myself in the head. I wasn't normally this bad with girls. I wasn't the prom king in high school or anything, but I was sure I had days when I could also turn heads and possibly break hearts.

Of course, Freyjn was most definitely in an entirely different higher level. Well out of my league. She was from another realm altogether. All the men she knew from there probably looked like the hottest Hollywood actors on Earth. She probably had them all lining up to kiss her hand, sharpen her daggers.

Whereas I was just a regular, weak human boy.

I pushed those unsettling thoughts out of my head as we trudged up the stairs at Erin's boyfriend's apartment building.

Loud party music with a deep bass line reverberated through the walls even all the way down the hall when we arrived on the third floor. Raucous laughter and cheery chattering overwhelmed my ears as we got closer to the already open door.

Erin must have spotted us the moment we walked through the door. Wearing a plaid yellow tailored ensemble, a thick headband pulling back her blonde hair, she came barrelling down the entryway, nearly tackling me with a hug. "Josh!"

"Hey!" I patted her back, making a face as I realized. "I forgot to get you a gift."

Erin's jaw dropping, she thumped on my chest. "What? What kind of idiot comes empty-handed to a birthday party? You're such a doof." She gave me an up-and-down assessing look. "Love the 'Grease' leather jacket look though. Wrong decade, but I love it!" Then her gaze slid over to Freyjn, "Oh, hello!" and turned to me, her eyes wide. "Josh, I didn't know you finally got a girlfriend!"

I almost scoffed.

I supposed the 'joke' had gone from surprising, to annoying, to amusing by now. I even thought I caught Freyjn stifling her chuckle beside me.

Almost grinning myself, I smacked Erin in the back of the head. "Shut up. You can't just assume that stuff."

Erin looked from Freyjn to me again. "Oh, she's not?" She frowned. "Aww, Mom would have been so happy!"

Rolling my eyes, I gestured nonchalantly to my fuchsia companion. "Erin, this is Freyjn. She's just a friend."

But Freyjn wasn't interested in pleasantries. Her eyes were already locked on to the long table laden with snacks a mere few feet away. There were towers of eclairs, bowls of candy, pretzels, a sandwich platter, assorted chips and dips, pitchers of juice, and several other bottles of drinks.

"Um, a really hungry friend," I added, gesturing for Freyjn to feel free to head over to get something to eat. She was gone so fast, I almost chuckled again.

Amused, Erin's eyebrow was raised. "*Just* a friend?"

"Yes," I replied pointedly, before giving her a puzzled look. "Besides, I thought you said Mom dragged some poor woman here to the party to set her up with me. Wasn't that why you insisted that I come tonight?"

"Oh! Well..." Erin's eyes sparkled with mischief. She pursed her lips. "The truth is..." Her eyes catching something across the room, she waved her hand as if to beckon someone over.

When Erin's boyfriend, Steven, arrived, he slid his arm around her shoulder. "Oh, hey, Josh, you made it," he greeted with a smile. He was wearing a long-sleeved plaid shirt and relaxed-fit jeans—to match Erin's '*Cher*' look from that 90s rom-com film.

"Steve, I'm telling him now," Erin told him.

I blinked. "Tell me what?"

With the biggest, widest, happiest smile, Erin yelled in my face, "We're engaged!"

My eyes bulged. "What?" I glanced from her to Steven, who was grinning from ear to ear. My smile widened. "That's-that's—oh, you guys! Congratulations!" I turned to hug Erin again, at the same time that I thumped on Steven's back.

"There was no girlfriend set up from Mom," Erin confessed as she pulled away. "Steve and I actually sent Mom away on a cruise with Rog, so they could relax and celebrate my happy news by themselves. I mean, she was going nuts excited." She gave me a knowing look. "You know how she gets. And I just wanted to make sure you were here for our special announcement."

I shook my head. "Wow. This is amazing. I'm so happy for you. Well, it's about time anyway, isn't it? You guys have been together for a while."

"You know." Steven shrugged, matter-of-factly. "I knew I'd better lock that down. Erin's the best thing that's ever happened to me."

Erin leaned up to kiss him on the cheek. "Baby, you're so sweet."

I made another face. "Oh jeez, please, no PDA in front of big bro."

"I think we need a toast or something," Steven piped up and turned to go first. "I'll get us some drinks."

Erin gazed up at me. "So you approve?"

I was only half-surprised. "Erin, you don't need my approval."

She shifted in her stance. "But you've always been, you know, like the man of the house...since Dad died. Or really even before that, since, you know..."

My expression sobered. "I just want you to be happy. If you love Steven and he makes you happy, you really don't need anyone else's approval."

Erin squeezed me in another hug. "You're the best big brother ever."

Something at the buffet table behind me caught Erin's attention and I glanced over my shoulder.

Handfuls of pretzels cupped in her hand, Freyjn was already chewing when she stopped to watch the chocolate fountain, seemingly completely mesmerized. Then one by one, she systematically swiped a piece of food across the stream to then taste—chunks of fruit, handfuls of Doritos, rolls of sushi—which when she put in her mouth, made her cringe and spit.

I bit back an amused chuckle.

But then after a moment, Freyjn slowed her chewing as if in deep thought—then she tried the chocolate sushi all over again.

Erin laughed behind her hand. She beamed wide eyes up at me. "I like your new girlfriend. Seems like she could put up with your particular brand of crazy."

I had to roll my eyes again. "More like she's bringing her own brand of crazy." I stopped short. "Also, again, she's *not* my girlfriend." I threw my hands up in the air. "Why is everyone so fixated that I make her my girlfriend?"

Erin leveled her gaze on me in mock disbelief. "Do you not see your face?" She poked my chest. "Dude, I noticed it the moment you came in. You looked happy. You finally look happy, Josh."

A bit off balance by the sincerity in her eyes, I shifted my stance. "What? I always look like this," I pointed out in my defense.

"Nuh-uh, big bro." Erin shook her head, her lips pursed.

I could tell she was about to school me.

"It's like...I feel like you've spent the last few years, I don't know—" She shrugged. "Waiting for something," she finished. "It's almost been like you're not really here. Or...that you'd rather be somewhere else, you know?" She elbowed me, a cheery grin back on her face. "But seeing you with this girl today...it's like a miracle." Her eager eyes shone up at me. "Is she who you were waiting for? Have you finally found her? You know, Mom and I would just really like for you to settle down, if that's what makes you happy."

My gaze settled on Freyjn again. She was at the make-your-own-sundae station holding a bowl of only toppings, licking what looked like fudge sauce from her fingertips.

There was no denying I was attracted to Freyjn. *Come on, who wouldn't be?* No denying Freyjn's smile made my stomach all weird and fluttery. She was just so...beautiful. And brave. And strong. And funny—if, unintentionally.

The disco lights glimmered in her long, pink hair. Her violet eyes were still wide. Everything at this party amazed her—which was the point in fact.

Erin had no idea what she was talking about.

She had no idea, for example, that Freyjn was from a mystical magical otherworld and that as soon as her quest on Earth was complete, she was going to disappear from my life forever.

I couldn't help a big sigh.

My sister tilted her head, studying my face. "Okay, that was one hell of a big sigh." She covered her mouth again, eyes wide in concern. "Oh gosh, maybe I shouldn't have said anything. Did you ask her out already and she rejected you? Are you being friend-zoned right now? Oh god, I'm so sorry."

I just groaned again. "A good sister is supposed to butt out of her big brother's love life."

Erin's laughter was merry, but it appeared she conceded my point. "Fine." She moved to thump on my back. "Well then, instead, why don't you be a good big brother and help me restock the cooler?" She gestured across the way. "The six-packs are in the big box in the other room, under the bar table."

Eyebrow furrowed, I cast a glance over at Freyjn.

Erin read my concern right away. "I'll keep an eye on her, don't worry," she assured me with a wink.

12

Chapter Twelve - Flashes

I wasn't gone two minutes, but when I came back out, I already couldn't help my instant frown.

Erin broke off from a conversation with a friend to jump toward me as I refilled the cooler with room-temp beer and soda, tucking the cans between large blocks of ice.

"Yay, thanks, Josh!" Stopping short from gushing, she craned her neck. "What are you glaring at?"

I blinked to neutralize my expression. "Glaring? I'm not glaring."

Erin followed my gaze toward the buffet table.

Some guy manifesting 'Garth Algar' in costume with a wiry white hair wig was now talking to Freyjn.

Check that, *flirting*—he was flirting with her.

So much for Erin keeping an eye on her.

Of course, this probably wasn't the type of trouble Erin was expecting to have to keep Freyjn away from.

My sister's shoulders were already shaking in amusement. "That's just Amos. He's a total wuss, but he does try hard."

I clenched my jaw. Another twinge constricted in me, starting to burn hot when Amos lifted his hand to casually touch Freyjn's elbow.

Erin was peering up at me. "Come on, you totally are glaring," she pointed out. "I thought you said she wasn't your girlfriend?"

"That's not the point, Erin. I'm pretty sure Freyjn doesn't appreciate being hit on right now by some random stranger."

Freyjn's eyes were narrowed. It could have been puzzlement, could have been displeasure. Either way, the heavy pressure in my chest wanted to give way to a sudden urge to stalk over and swoop in to take her away.

But before I could act on my urge, Freyjn moved so fast, I barely saw it.

The next thing Erin and I saw was Amos's pained face, pressed down against the table, his arm twisted behind his back in Freyjn's vise-like grip.

She leaned over him to whisper something near his ear. But from the way Amos' eyes widened in terror, I could guess it wasn't anything friendly.

Erin started wheezing her laughter, slapping my back several times in total amusement. "I-I—she just—I can't believe—"

The stinging inside me instead grew to burgeoning warmth. Was it pleasure? Could have been pride or maybe amazement overall. Freyjn did say she could take care of herself.

A second guy, this time dressed like 'Wayne', approached Freyjn and Amos, possibly to diffuse the situation.

Shaking my head, I strode across the room anyway, in case the warrior princess planned to put both of these poor boys into a chokehold. Or at least I could steer any others clear or warn them away or something.

Amos had straightened up, nursing his arm, while his friend was trying to talk amiably with Freyjn. "Sorry about this guy. He does have a tendency to run his mouth, Miss...?"

Arriving at her side, I cut in before Freyjn could respond. "Hey, babe. Are these guys bothering you?"

Freyjn's gaze snapped up to me in surprise.

Amos and his friend both looked panicked for some reason. "S-sorry, sir." Amos stammered as they both scrambled away.

Curious, I tilted my head to watch them leave. They were Erin's age, friends from school. Sure, I was a few years older than them, but their reaction seemed a tad bit extreme. Why did they look so scared? "That's weird."

Freyjn was frowning up at me again.

I blinked. "What? Why are you staring at me like that?"

"Your eyes," she mumbled, studying me closely. "I thought I saw..."

"Saw what?"

"Nothing. Never mind." Freyjn averted her gaze. "Did you just call me 'babe'? Like an infant?"

I blinked. "Oh, that's not what I meant. I was just trying to—um, 'babe' is like a term of endearment, like, here in this realm."

If I was any smoother, I would have asked her if she'd liked it. A shiver shot up my spine at the mere thought. Instead, I cleared my throat to dismiss that stir in my stomach once again. "I was just messing with those kids. Don't worry about it."

Glancing over at the buffet table, I pursed my lips in amusement. "So, are you enjoying the party? Looks like you've acquainted yourself quite well with the food in this realm."

She merely glared up at me.

For a change, it didn't send a nervous chill down my spine. I was starting to get used to her glares. Hiding my grin, I opened my can of soda and took a swig, but I forgot it was still warm. I made a face in distaste. "Mm."

Freyjn's attention was elsewhere, occupied inspecting the freshly-refilled antipasti platter.

I tilted my head in thought. "Hey."

She turned her head the slightest amount in my direction but gave no other indication that she was listening.

Glancing furtively around to make sure nobody else could see, I held out the soda can to her. "If it doesn't summon those warriors again...could you do that ice thing again with this?"

Without a word, Freyjn reached out with a finger to tap on the base of the can.

I barely blinked and the entire can frosted white all over. "Whoa." I took another sip and murmured in pleasure at the now-icy cold drink. "Oh, that's much better. Thanks."

Freyjn's gaze turned forlorn as she eyed the food.

The way she practically wilted made my chest all heavy. My eyebrows furrowed in concern. "Something wrong?"

Shaking her head, she wrapped her arms around herself.

I moved closer to ask, "Are you sensing danger again?

"No."

I cast a furtive glance around the noisy party. Erin and Steven's friends were still having the time of their lives, chattering, laughing, and throwing popcorn. Nothing looked even remotely suspicious.

I gave her an up-and-down assessing look. Was she still worried about that doofus Amos? Maybe she sensed the threat posed by the seemingly drunken guys roughhousing near the balcony. "Is it getting uncomfortable for you here now? Do you want to leave?"

"No."

Loud whooping overlay the pop disco hits blaring from someone's Spotify playlist. Some kids had pushed back the coffee table and chairs for a makeshift dance floor.

I desperately wanted to cheer her up. I pursed my lips. "Do you want to...dance?"

Those violet eyes widened as they fixed right up at me.

She didn't blink for like thirty seconds, didn't answer, didn't say anything.

My heart was already in my throat. I set my drink down. I gently nudged the small of her back to lead her toward the center of the room before turning her to me to whisper, "Is this okay?"

I caught the most subtle of nods, but a flush of warmth spread through me anyway.

Taking her one hand in mine, I slid my other hand across her back. The silky fabric of her dress was cool beneath my fingers as I tugged her a bit closer.

Her breath caught in a gasp.

To be honest, mine also did.

I took one step left, and then back, leading her into an easy box step. I didn't care at all that we were completely out of sync with the rhythm of the latest Dua Lipa song. Not when the girl of my dreams was gazing up at me like that, as if in complete awe.

This isn't a date.

Shut up, Josh.

I shuffled closer to her—totally an accident. Another couple bumped into me from behind. That fragrant scent was making me heady again.

No other girl ever had this effect on me, from one mere silly dance, or by simply standing near me.

I felt like I was back in my dream. My head was going hazy, my eyelids heavy.

I wanted to keep her in my arms, pull her in tighter, dip my head lower so I could get lost in that scent, in this feeling...

A rush of images flooded my mind.

I was holding Freyjn, her back pressed against my body, much like when I'd caught her earlier today before she attempted to cross at that red light.

Except, we weren't in the middle of a busy city street.

We were in a dark, thick forest of green, green trees.

My heart was still pounding like I had just been running for my life. A cacophony of exhilaration, panic, and concern swirled around inside my body, inside my head.

Freyjn had collapsed in my arms.

Why? I wondered.

She was gazing up at me, tired, but relieved, almost in wonder.

My breath caught in my throat when I thought her entire body glimmered for a moment.

It happened so fast, I couldn't be sure, before a thick fog swept in—white, almost blinding... giving way to...something else...

Of brightness and fire, a mighty swish, followed by a sudden rush of wind. Something large. And powerful. I felt engulfed by it, as if it surrounded me, tightened around me...

And I couldn't breathe.

The sudden surge of the vision almost struck me like a physical blow.

I gasped when I opened my eyes, not realizing I'd closed them.

My pulse racing, I blinked like a million times as I looked around.

We were still at Erin's party, at Steven's apartment, the same noise, the same dimmed lights, the same crowd.

I'd just had some sort of hallucination—hazy, but intense at the same time.

But what the actual hell even was all that?

It almost felt like what I usually saw whenever I dreamed of her, except it was more vivid. It was like I'd actually been to that forest with her before. Like all of that had really happened.

Did Freyjn make me see those visions? Why?

I didn't realize I'd braced my hands on Freyjn's arms either. I shot her a confused look. But before I could open my mouth to ask, I noticed she was also shaking herself. She looked just as disoriented.

Catching my gaze, she caught my own flash of bewilderment.

No.

It wasn't her. *She* didn't do that.

Trying to catch her breath, Freyjn dropped her gaze. "I need some air."

13

Chapter Thirteen - Human

The cool night breeze washed over my overheated skin as soon as we reached the sidewalk outside Steven's building.

Her tone urgent, her eyes full wide, Freyjn turned to me. "You saw that too, didn't you? When we danced?"

Too? I could only nod.

It was late and the neighborhood was relatively quiet. The glistening black pavement, slick with recent rain, mirrored the glow of the streetlights in fractured, shimmering streaks.

She rubbed her forehead. "I don't understand."

I swallowed hard. "I thought your magic was doing that to me. Is the oath making me see visions?"

Her eyebrows were deeply furrowed. "I'm not sure. It doesn't usually work that way." Shivering, she ran her hands up her bare arms.

"Oh." Jumping, I shrugged off my jacket to drape around her shoulders. "Is that better?" When my hands brushed against hers as she pulled the jacket closer, my skin tingled.

This couldn't all just be a coincidence.

"Look." I gave her a steady look. "I don't know about you, and I hope this doesn't sound weird, but..." I paused, trying to find the right words. "I've been...feeling this thing about you all day."

Her one eyebrow rose.

I hurried to correct myself. "I mean—" I wrung my hands out. "I don't know how to explain it. It's like...I feel like I know you. Maybe not that we've met before necessarily, but that I *know* you. Is that possible? Like, maybe it's a previous life thing?"

"It's not possible."

I heaved a helpless sigh, having figured out absolutely nothing. If it wasn't her magic that was causing these feelings, that caused that vision, then what?

I chewed on the insides of my cheeks. "Are we sure we saw the same vision? What did you see? Maybe together, we can figure out what it means."

"It means nothing." She spun to dismiss me, hurrying down the street. "It means—we should be getting back to the mission."

I jumped to catch up with her. "Do you think maybe the vision was something that's about to happen? Can your magic predict the future?" I paused again. Except the Freyjn in the vision did look a tad bit younger than the Freyjn that was trying to run ahead of me.

So did that mean it was in the *past*?

I was struggling to catch my breath. Man, this girl could run. I was about to yell at her to slow down when she screeched to a stop so suddenly, I almost ran into her.

"What are you..." I trailed off when I noticed where her gaze had distracted toward.

One of the menacing warrior dudes from the amusement park earlier stepped out of the shadows right ahead.

Uh-oh.

"Maybe we shouldn't have left that party," I mumbled, pushing past Freyjn's immobile form so I could stand in the way.

When the warrior dude spoke, his voice was less raspy than I was expecting. Of course, it wasn't less threatening. "Stand aside, boy. We are just here for the girl."

'*Regular weak human boy...*' echoed in my head and I gritted my teeth. I held my hand out to keep Freyjn behind me, trying to exude as much confidence as I could despite my nerves. "Oh, yeah? Why don't you try and come at me?"

Casting a glance around, I hid my sigh in relief.

There was only one of him—so far. The rest of the menacing horde was probably scattered throughout the city trying to sniff us out.

The warrior gave me a dark, mocking look before stalking over without hesitation.

Uh-oh.

Admittedly, I was only half-bluffing. I wanted to prove I could hold my own against at least one of them, but the adrenaline pumping through my veins was also triggering my flight reflex.

I pushed Freyjn ahead to run away before turning to make a break for it. But the thug moved faster than humanly possible and he caught me from behind.

"Aagh!"

The warrior wound his arm encircling my neck in a chokehold.

My vision immediately blurred as blood rushed to my head.

Holy crap! My heart pounded in my ears. I flailed to struggle free even as I desperately gasped for air. I clutched at my throat, coughing, attempting to loosen his freaking vise-like grip.

Like a nightmare, three more menacing warriors popped out of nowhere to engage Freyjn. One of them grabbed her from behind. Just as quickly as she'd disarmed Amos, Freyjn whipped around to kick him off her. But there were another two of them and more on the way.

Freyjn was going to get captured.

No! I gritted my teeth.

Dammit.

Even as I struggled against my captor's grip, I racked my brain to remember those self-defense technique videos floating around on the internet.

Squeezing my eyes in concentration, I planted my feet firmly on the ground then thrust my elbow back in the warrior's ribs—hard.

He grunted from the force. When his grip faltered slightly, I twisted my body to wrench out from under his hold.

Finally breaking free, and with a strength I absolutely had no idea I had, I grabbed his arm—yes, the big, monstrous thug guy—and yanked him up and over my shoulder, to come slamming down on the cracked pavement with a thunderous crash.

My own jaw dropped as I stared at the fallen warrior on the ground.

What the—?

How did I even manage that?

Except I really shouldn't have kept standing there amazed.

Another one of the dark warrior thugs was already advancing from the shadows, as if it was dispensing them, his menacing arms already reaching out for me.

"Oh, shoot!" I scrambled back—a failed attempt to best his seriously inhuman speed.

The ghost of his grip brushed so close to my throat again, but then the warrior stopped dead in his tracks.

With a grunt, the thug grabbed at his own neck. As if he couldn't breathe himself, as if some invisible force was choking him too.

My eyes bulged as his entire hulky form rose a few feet off the ground.

What the hell—?

My heart hammered.

How on Earth was this all happening?

"Are you done almost getting caught yet?"

The twinge in my chest was relief at the wry tone and I turned to look.

My fuchsia fairy was glowing again, not two steps behind me. She hadn't abandoned me. Her hands were raised, wielding her magic, while that mysterious wind whipped up and down the length of the street.

I couldn't help my eyes widening in awe.

Violet mist burst from Freyjn's form, the wind lashing at her hair, at her dress. Her feet were braced apart in determination as she stood in the middle of the alleyway. Her sharp eyes glimmered amidst the shimmer of the streets.

Damn.

The warrior clutched at his throat.

Helpless. Defenseless.

Letting out a breath in relief, I couldn't help a grin—short-lived, as more of those dark warriors materialized from the darkness all around us.

Dread churned in my stomach. No doubt Freyjn's magic was acting like a beacon once again, telling them exactly where to find us.

I held my hand out to her. "Let's get out of here."

The warrior she was choking collapsed with a clatter onto the pavement, as with a quick nod, Freyjn moved to take my hand so we could rabbit out of there.

The silence of the nearly deserted streets was broken only by the slap of our footsteps against the concrete. Rhythmic footfalls of our pursuers echoed like a death knell, steady and relentless behind us.

We dashed down the street toward the junction of the train station and dodged through the turnstiles, even with the heavy marching boots blending with the metallic clanging and the chugging of the rail transit line as it whooshed past.

"Plan?" Freyjn shot a wary glance over her shoulder.

"Up the stairs. Trust me."

I led the way up the staircase leading into the fluorescent-lit cavern. Halfway up, I grabbed Freyjn's arm, yanking her toward the railing, and we vaulted over the rail together, landing on the lower staircase in a crouch.

"Shh," I murmured, pulling Freyjn into the shadows. She pressed close, gripping my arm for balance.

I blew out a breath of relief as the thugs thundered past us above. With any luck, they might think we managed to hop on that train that just left.

I signaled Freyjn to follow me down the stairs once again, slipping out of the station, and darting into another narrow alley between what looked like old, abandoned warehouses.

For a moment, the silence returned, broken only by our labored breathing.

Glancing surreptitiously around us, I led the way down the darkened streets. "I think we lost the bad guys."

"I never said they were bad guys," Freyjn corrected. "I just said they were from my realm trying to capture me to bring me back."

I stopped short. "Wait, what? Are you kidding me right now? You mean, they're not actually evil? They're not trying to kill us?"

"Well, I know they're not trying to kill me," she huffed.

WHAT?

My brain almost exploded. I almost willingly sprawled facedown on the dirty streets in exhaustion. What had we been running from them all the live long day for?

"Oh—oh, that's just great." I did my *millionth* facepalm. "So what, do you actually know these guys? Are they under your command or something? Why were you killing them off?"

She pursed her lips. "I don't command them and I didn't kill them. I merely incapacitated them. You missed the point. They're trying to stop me from completing my mission."

"It sounds more like they just want you to come back home safe and sound." I dropped my head. "Oh, great, I've been preventing them from bringing you home safely." I pulled on her hand to walk backward. "That's it. I knew there could have been a way to just talk to these guys. They're not going to stop until you get back home."

Shrugging out of my grasp, Freyjn cried out, "I cannot go home! I must find the one bearing the mark. The fate of my realm depends on it!" Her eyes shone with fervor.

Oh, shoot. Was she...holding back tears?

"Everyone is relying on me to do this. This is my only chance to prove—" She stopped short to turn away, folding her arms across her chest, as if to compose herself.

I pursed my lips at her outburst.

She really was desperate. Whatever this mission was, to her, it was a really *big* deal.

Ah, dammit.

I let out a long drawn-out resigned sigh. "Alright, alright," I soothed, patting her back. I didn't want her to cry. "Jeez. Look, for what it's worth. I think it's great how committed you are to this. I mean, at least you know your purpose. Besides, I already swore some binding magical oath to help you. You know I can't get out of it. But I would just appreciate knowing all the details. You haven't even told me much about why I'm risking my life right now. I mean, how can I protect you if you keep secrets from me?"

Over her shoulder, she glared at me again. "*You* protect me?"

I shot her an almost offended look. "Hey, in case you didn't notice, you're still here freely terrorizing my life, instead of being dragged back to your realm by those goons—*thus far.*"

I was about to go on to congratulate myself on our continuously cleverly escaping our pursuers when two more menacing warrior figures emerged from the mouth of the alley, followed by two more, and then even more, their shadows stretching long in the faint streetlight.

Freyjn's gasp caught in her throat.

When I turned to the other side, another group of them was approaching us from the opposite end of the street. My shoulders tensed at the grim expression on their faces. "There's even more of them than before."

Maybe there could have been a slim chance of talking with them earlier today, but I had a sneaking suspicion, the time for negotiations was over.

Freyjn was already shaking her head. I could tell her mind was still spinning, thinking what to do, struggling to come up with a way out of this.

I bit my lip, glancing up and down the alley.

My eyes caught the fire escape ladder across the way. But before the notion fully formed in my head, a figure crashed through the windows of the building beside us.

Startled, I jumped to shield Freyjn from the shards of glass that went flying about. "Watch out!"

I squinted at the sudden bright blinding light for a moment. It appeared as a spherical shield surrounding us, protecting us from the menacing warriors.

Following the trail of magic, I peered up at the dark figure who was hopefully a powerful sorcerer stepping in at the exact right moment to save us.

His back was to us, one hand thrust out to summon the mystical shield. But when he glanced over his shoulder to check that we were okay, I was so shocked, I almost lost control of my bodily fluids.

His coat was dirty and torn, possibly from that crazy stunt of jumping through that window there. His face was scruffy, bearded—but with those familiar dark green eyes, I knew would recognize him anywhere.

My jaw dropped in wild disbelief. "D-Dad...?"

14

Chapter Fourteen - Surprise

"**S**tay back." Frank Richards gestured us down with one hand (while his other hand was somehow keeping hold conjuring some type of magical shield to keep away those menacing warriors from another realm and—WHAT? What the damn hell was going on?)

I couldn't move from the shock.

My dad was alive.

He was alive.

He saved us and he was alive.

And he was...magic...?

I still couldn't snap my mouth shut in bewildering disbelief.

My dad waved his arms and a giant ball of light exploded.

Once the darkness fell again, each of the dozen or so warriors dropped with a clatter to the ground.

My dad let out a breath, straightening in his stance before turning to us. "Are you two okay?"

My limbs felt frozen in my crouch. I almost thought I was going to pass out altogether.

Freyjn had to tug on my arm to get me up standing.

A deep crease on his forehead, my dad strode over, the streetlights silhouetting his form.

My brain was whirling with so many questions, but the first one that popped out was, "A-are they dead?"

My dad shook his head. "No. I don't do that." He cast Freyjn a prompting look. "Have you depleted your magic?"

Freyjn glanced down at her hands. "Not yet."

"Ha-Hang on a minute." I rubbed my temples. I really felt like my brain was about to explode. "I don't understand what's going on. Do you two know each other?" I motioned from my dad to Freyjn.

Giving me a pointed look, Freyjn shook her head.

"No," my dad replied. "But I recognize the magic of the Priori people of Arcadia." He tilted his head. "I am at your service."

Freyjn acknowledged with a mere nod. "I wasn't aware there were other mages from my realm here. I appreciate your assistance, but I am on an urgent mission. We must be on our way." She tugged on my arm to lead me away.

"The person you are looking for isn't here."

Freyjn stopped short at my dad's declaration. Slowly, she turned to give him a narrow-eyed look.

Heck, I was still staring at him, gobsmacked.

Did he know who the hell she was looking for? Also, how on earth could he possibly know who the *hell* she was looking for?

My dad's tone was even, steady. "I've hidden him." He cast a glance around. "But it is too risky to venture into the city now. I shall take you to him tomorrow."

What in the—? Okay. Not only did my dad know exactly who Freyjn was looking for, but apparently, he'd even hidden him—as if my dad was in charge, as if he knew everything, as if he'd known everything all along.

I buried my face in my hands. "I think I need to lie down."

Nodding, my dad beckoned with his arm. "Follow me."

Honestly, I barely registered getting up. I let Freyjn lead me to follow my dad down the alley. I couldn't stop shaking my head.

My dad was alive.

No, no. My dad was an irresponsible selfish jerk who'd left my family years ago and then died shortly thereafter. Complications from acute heart failure. I'd seen the casket myself.

Didn't I...?

My dad led us down a back alleyway, past several massive, windowless buildings.

Stagnant salty water mingled with the oil and decaying wood. Water sloshed against creaking wood, punctuated by the occasional clanging of a buoy.

We neared a seemingly disused warehouse standing stark against the inky black water. It was the place Freyjn had seen from on top of the Ferris wheel, the place near the docks.

When my dad pulled the large railed door, it opened with a loud chug.

From the outside, the windows were all boarded up, a few broken glass panes reflecting what little light the streetlights offered. The inside was only slightly more impressive—a wide, open-plan industrial space, sparsely furnished.

"We should be safe here for tonight." My dad collapsed with a sigh onto the sofa set in front of a recycled coffee table. There was a functional kitchen to one side and up the metal staircase to the left appeared to be a small loft.

Highly intrigued, I looked around. "Do you live here?"

Wait.

I almost forgot about my outrage.

I whirled to face him. "I mean, who the *hell* are you?" With a brisk shake of my head, I burst out, "What the *hell* is going on? I thought you died! You were supposed to have died years ago! How are you even alive?" I threw up my hands in severe disbelief. "And how on Earth do you have magic? How do you even know *anything* about this?"

Both my dad and Freyjn merely stared at me.

My shoulders heaving, I tried to catch my breath. My head was still whirling but it felt good to at least have gotten that out.

Not even fazed, my dad straightened up from the couch. He gestured to Freyjn. "Why don't you get her settled upstairs to get some rest first? That sofa bed sticks a bit, almost like the one we used to have. Then you and I can talk."

I nodded, subdued. I motioned Freyjn to walk ahead of me up the stairs.

The loft was minimally furnished, sofa bed, standing lamp. I kicked the bottom of the sofa, rattled the latch a couple of times, and it popped open just like my dad had said. I couldn't even believe he remembered that minor detail about our old couch at home.

Turning her around, I helped Freyjn shrug off my jacket then turned down the sofa bed for her. At least it looked comfortable.

Or at least, Freyjn didn't complain when she slipped under the covers.

Still lost in thought, I mechanically set to tucking her in. "You need to stay warm," I murmured, leaning over to pull the blankets up.

"Josh?"

I stopped, finding my face hovering above hers—almost too closely. That was the first time she'd spoken my name. When my gaze involuntarily dropped to her mouth, my pulse raced back to life. "Yes?"

"You saved my life today."

I shrugged. "Three times but who's counting?"

Those red lips curved into a soft smile. "I only counted two."

When I met her eyes again, those violet depths sparkled in the dim light. It seemed as though she was going to say something more, but then she hesitated.

Feeling a little bold, I moved to press a kiss to her forehead, tucking her hair behind her ear. That fragrant scent filled my lungs and there was another stir in my stomach... An aching, perhaps some sort of deep longing. It made absolutely no sense.

Before I was tempted to drop any more kisses on her face, her eyelids, her nose, that tempting one corner of that sassy mouth... I pulled away to head back downstairs.

Halfway down, I braced myself against the stairway railing to catch my breath, settle my nerves. Everything today was one rollercoaster after another—emotional or otherwise. And the day wasn't even over yet.

His back to me, my dad was in the kitchen, setting a couple of mugs down on the counter beside a boiling kettle. "Coffee?"

I almost groaned in relief. "God, yes, please."

As if none of this was anything out of the ordinary, he poured the golden brown liquid and turned to smile at me. "How was Erin's birthday?"

Those familiar eyes, that rare, warm smile. Exactly the way I remembered my dad when I was younger.

Furrowing my eyebrows in frustration, I blew out a breath. "What the hell, Dad? How could you not have told us you were still alive, and still in New York? Did you fake your own death? I mean, come on! Mom was—was—well, it wasn't good!"

He pursed his lips. "I'm sorry, son, but it was necessary. If it makes you feel any better, I've been watching over you all since." He held out the cup of coffee for me.

I was still shaking my head as I took it. "I just...I can't believe any of this is happening. I mean, I already couldn't believe it when some fairy showed up in my apartment this morning and basically blackmailed me to help her out, but now you're here—and you're...magic?"

I took a sip from my cup and the bitter, hot drink slid down my throat.

It sure tasted like coffee.

I squeezed my eyes shut for a moment.

Maybe I was having another episode. Maybe none of this was actually real. What were the odds that I was just having another really vivid, really weird dream?

I groaned. "Is any of this really happening? Or am I going crazy? Again?"

When my dad met my gaze, his eyebrows were raised slightly. "Again?" he repeated. "Are you referring to that time a few years ago when you lost your memories?"

I nodded. "It was right after you died—I mean, after we thought you had died. Everyone thought I was just traumatized, that it was a nervous breakdown or psychological episode caused by stress."

Seemingly warming both hands on his own cup of coffee, my dad took a seat on the couch, gesturing for me to do the same. "It is not the time to tell you all the details, but rest assured, everything I have done has all been to keep you safe."

When he spoke again, his tone was completely matter-of-fact. "Josh. It was me. I took your memories."

15

Chapter Fifteen - Villains

I woke up with that heaviness still weighing on my chest. I was entirely not surprised to wake up on the couch, staring at the bare ceiling of the dank warehouse that my dad had led that pink fairy and me to last night after getting attacked by all the magical warriors from another world.

Too many bombshells, even the stiffest cup of coffee couldn't keep my exhausted brain awake last night, so my dad decided I should sleep it off first too before we dug deeper into any more explanations.

Faint daylight streamed in through the gaps in the boarded-up windows. Dishes clanking from the kitchen drew my gaze.

Both my dad and Freyjn were already up, having a quiet discussion over the sink, possibly more about otherworldly concerns.

Glancing back, Freyjn noticed me awake first.

"Oh." My dad turned with a smile. "Good. You're awake. There's toast, cereal, oatmeal, and honey for breakfast if you want to freshen up first." He gestured to the door to one side which must have been the bathroom.

My eyes widened first. "Oatmeal and honey? You're kidding."

Oatmeal and honey, just like my dad used to make. I seriously didn't know whether to laugh or cry.

I shoved those thoughts out of my mind and went to wash up—at least, that was a routine I could still depend on.

My dad had stocked up on spare toothbrushes, toothpaste, toilet paper, and hand towels. I almost had to wonder if this was actually a 'safe house', and maybe my dad was hiding from the law, or he was a spy, or a secret agent, or something. Well, no, of course. He was some sort of 'mage' from a mystical other world.

Coming out of the bathroom, I looked around in the daylight at the furniture, the electricity, the running water. "Hey, *Dad*," I mused aloud. "How are you even paying for all this when you're supposed to be dead?"

My dad's chuckle was throaty as he went about washing dishes. "You never knew this, kid, but you get your resourcefulness streak from your father."

Well, heck. It seemed like I knew nothing about my dad at all.

Freyjn was waiting by the toaster, head inclined, nails rhythmically tapping on the fake granite. That long bright pink hair hung down her back, cascading over her bare shoulders. I was almost tempted to brush it to one side, run my fingers through the silky mass.

Wake up, Josh. You're still dreaming.

Clearing my throat as I came up beside her, I gave her shoulder a slight nudge. "Did you sleep okay?" I asked, under my breath.

Freyjn almost looked surprised at my quiet greeting, but she nodded.

There were questions in those violet eyes.

I wondered if she was going to tear me a new one for that forehead kiss last night.

My head being much clearer this morning, I realized I probably shouldn't have done that. Or more accurately, I *definitely* shouldn't have done that.

She was absolutely not my girlfriend.

She would never be my girlfriend. Not in three thousand years.

She wasn't even from this world.

I knew it was completely crazy to get too attached. Even as I tamped down that nagging voice in the back of my head saying 'Oh, you idiot. It's so too late for that.'

The toaster popped with a ping.

I gave her a half-smile as I handed her the piece of toast.

Freyjn opened her mouth as if she wanted to say something. But after a moment, she simply turned back to my dad. She blinked a few times. "What were we talking about?"

My dad had an amused smirk on his mouth. "The person you were looking for..."

"Right." She blinked again, as if snapping to attention. "And you're sure you know where he is?" Her expression intense, eager, she went to sit down across from him on the easy chair.

"Yes." My dad nodded. "I've been keeping him safe all this time."

Scratching my head, I walked to the pantry. "Right, so can someone please tell me now? Who are we looking for? Who is this guy, exactly?"

Freyjn fidgeted in her seat. "Where I am from, he is called the 'Curse Bearer'. My mission is to find him. He is the key to saving my realm. He will awaken the magic long sleeping and bring hope to my people. It has all been foretold."

"Great." Shrugging, I helped myself to the food. Except, as usual, nothing Freyjn said made any sense to me. Sleeping magic. Saving realms. Whatever else it was, whoever this guy was she was looking for, best of luck to him.

My dad was oddly quiet, merely sipping his coffee as he sank back in his seat.

Pulling out a stool with a screech at the counter, I mostly inhaled the breakfast food.

Taking out my phone, I happened to catch several more missed calls and about a dozen text messages from work right before the screen conked out altogether.

"Oh, shoot." I groaned, waving my phone in the air. "You got a phone charger here somewhere?"

"Ah, sorry, no." My dad shook his head. "That one I actually do not have."

"I have to call my boss." Quickly finishing up, I stood with a sigh. "He's probably worried I'm missing work two days in a row with no notice."

My dad's forehead creased. "I thought you hated that job anyway?"

I made a face. "I—" I stopped short. "Wait, how do *you* know I hate that job?"

"Son, I've been watching you for a while." He shrugged as stood up to start putting dirty dishes away. "The only reason I wasn't alerted right away to Freyjn's arrival was because she was...masked quite well."

I leaned against the counter. "Well, *Dad*, now that you're here, maybe you can take Freyjn to see this guy. You don't need me anymore, right? I can go back to work?"

My dad was already nodding. "He is right." He shot Freyjn an acquiescing look. "I can take you to the Curse Bearer. We don't need Josh any longer."

Freyjn's expression remained neutral. "The oath may disagree with you."

"What oath?" My dad's eyebrow shot up.

"Your son has sworn an oath to me, and until my task is complete, he is bound." Her statement was punctuated with a sip of her drink.

The disbelief on my dad's face when he turned to me was uncanny. "You did what?"

"What?" I grimaced. "How could I have possibly known what I was getting into?" I gave a big showy wave in his direction. "You know, this is all your fault. If you had told me all about your fake death and being magic and everything, maybe I would have been more careful swearing oaths to loathsome fairies."

Freyjn's jaw dropped in offense. "Hey!"

"Sorry." I rolled my eyes.

My dad gave Freyjn a prompting look. "Surely, you can let him off the hook now. I can help you finish your mission.

She tilted her chin up in complete authority. "I might still need him. He's proven to be very useful so far."

I couldn't help a scoff. "Oh, hey, at least thanks for acknowledging that."

Freyjn pursed her lips. "Either way, you are still sworn to me—until and unless I say so."

My dad just shook his head.

Last night's bright lights and awesome magic display aside, I had a sneaking suspicion that my dad's magic was in no way a match for the bright pink fairy's. And I think he knew it too.

I threw my hands up. "Alright, fine, then, this is ridiculous and I'm so sorry to ask, but I really have to pop by my office for a minute before going to find your Mr. Curse Bearer. My boss is already going berserk. Is that acceptable to my oath?"

Freyjn let out a long, drawn-out sigh. "I suppose." She met my dad's gaze. "If your father can guarantee access to the Curse Bearer, then I shall allow one last detour."

I put my hands together and gave her a bow. "Thank you, oh generous one."

I was sure it was already a ridiculous sight for me to be walking down the streets with my supposedly-deceased dad dressed in his dark, long trench coat like he was a covert hobo, and a weird, sullen fuchsia girl.

It was late in the morning, a bright, fine day in Brooklyn might I add. It wouldn't even rain so we could possibly have a chance at traveling incognito. Just my luck.

I was making an effort not to run into anyone I knew on the way, but as we turned the corner to the modest two-story building of the company where I worked, I caught sight of one of my female colleagues walking up from the other end of the street.

Oh, boy.

She was about my age, petite, blonde—hopefully not nosy or suspicious.

"Oh, hey, Emily." I greeted her first, giving her a half-awkward smile as she met us along the paved path leading up toward the building entrance.

One of Emily's eyebrows turned up as she noticed the two characters I was with, but she didn't break her gait and simply returned my smile. "Hey, Josh. Is everything okay? You've missed a few days this week, haven't you?"

I jumped ahead of her to get the door. "I'm fine. I'm just uh...having some family stuff."

Her gaze slid back to my dad and Freyjn again. "I see." She gave me a once-over look. "Hey, I love this leather jacket look on you. Very cool."

"Oh, thanks." My neck warmed at her compliment. "It's not really my usual style."

"But it looks great."

My dad was feigning nonchalance, or possibly genuine boredom, as he surreptitiously retreated beneath the cover of some shady trees across the way, but I could tell he was checking the immediate premises for threats.

A mere few steps behind me on the path, Freyjn was watching me and Emily with a glare of her own.

Pausing by the door I was holding open for her, Emily leaned closer to me. "Well, if you need any help running interference with Andrew, I'm always happy to do you a favor. You know you can count on me, right?"

Flushing red, I scratched my head. Good thing Emily was one of the rare ones among my colleagues with whom I actually got along. "Oh, thanks, Emily. I really appreciate that."

With another winning smile, Emily gave me a friendly wink before she headed inside.

Relieved she didn't ask any questions, I let the door swing shut behind Emily. I turned around and nearly jumped out of my skin. "Yow—!"

Her eyes narrowed, Freyjn was right behind me, peering over my shoulder as if in suspicion. "Who was that?"

Shifting in my stance, I shrugged. "One of my colleagues from work."

"One of your girlfriends?"

I almost choked. "What? No." Sighing in exasperation, I glanced from her to my dad. "You two stay out here. I'll just go check in with my boss."

"Are you sure you're going to be safe inside?" Freyjn piped up.

I shot her another look at the unexpected tinge of concern in her tone. "Um, unless your warrior friends decide to attack my work in broad daylight, I think I should be fine."

With a quiet huff, Freyjn averted her gaze. "I suppose you have more female colleagues who would be happy to do you favors."

"Sure..." I trailed off, staring at her in slight disbelief. Okay, what was her problem all of a sudden?

But Freyjn didn't meet my gaze again.

Resisting the urge to roll my eyes, I gestured toward the door. "I'm gonna go inside now. If I'm not back in fifteen minutes, well..." I shrugged. "Maybe my boss ate me." I put my hand up immediately when Freyjn whirled around in alarm. "Kidding."

Her face collapsed into another annoyed frown, but she merely folded her arms across her chest and stepped closer to my dad, in an attempt to blend in amongst the trees as well.

Neither of them looked happy to wait.

Well, neither of them looked happy. Period.

Fortunately for them, I was done inside in less than half an hour.

Literally "done."

In all honesty, I thought it would have taken longer.

The moment my boss Andrew had caught sight of me entering the bull pen, his entire face turned red and it was all downhill from there.

Talk about real-life villains.

On my way out, I passed Emily by the breakroom. Much like the rest of the people on the floor, she had heard everything.

She gave me a consoling pat on the arm. "You know you're better off," she said, under her breath. "A few of us were talking about it the other day. Andrew's going to have a massive walk-out on his hands soon. Sheila was thinking of starting her own firm. I'm sure we'll be in touch."

I gave her a half-hearted smile in return before turning to leave. She was probably right.

I even had a sneaking suspicion Andrew had been looking forward to this. It wasn't entirely implausible that he had only been waiting for the *one* day I would finally, royally screw up, in order to warrant my firing. It was just his luck that until yesterday before I met Freyjn and my life got turned upside-down, I was an exemplary employee.

Then again, maybe he just did me a favor.

I pushed past the building doors to head back outside. My shoulders slumped, hands shoved in my pockets. I trudged back toward my dad and Freyjn. "Well...I got fired."

"For missing two days of work?" my dad mused, his eyebrows raised. "Can your company really afford to let go of loyal, hardworking employees like that?"

I let out a big sigh. "My boss says I'm just not a team player and a know-it-all. He did a whole number about his doubts on whether I'll ever amount to anything."

Freyjn's jaw dropped. "What? That's ridiculous!"

"Meanwhile, Ron's back from Cancun on vacation, and because he claims he was greasing up customers, he can file it all under 'Client Acquisitions'." I shrugged. "I told you my boss is a jerk."

Her eyebrows snapped together, and taking a very determined step forward, she clasped her hands. "Do you want me to choke him?"

My eyes nearly popped out in alarm. "Oh, no, no, no, no—" I braced my hands on her arms to hold her back. "It's fine, it's fine." Pulling her to one side, I lowered my voice to a hiss, "And I told you, you shouldn't use your magic in front of people." I almost laughed at the incensed look on her face. "But thanks for the offer."

Freyjn looked more outraged than me. She shrugged my hands off to cross her arms over her chest again with a huff.

"So," my dad spoke up. "If that's all the detour we require, now can we get on with the mission?"

16

❧

Chapter Sixteen - Quest

The oddball trio of us fit in quite nicely with the mid-day Brooklyn subway crowd.

Across the aisle, a man in a full Captain America costume was sipping a milkshake, while a woman in a fur coat cradled an iguana like a baby.

My pink-haired fairy was sitting beside me. Her gaze fixed out the window, seemingly entranced by the intermittently changing view as the subway rattled along the elevated tracks.

The gray-blue expanse of the Atlantic gave way to dense neighborhoods dotted with stoops and fire escapes, cobblestone streets, and warehouses, while the skyline of Manhattan teased the horizon up ahead.

I glanced over at a guy playing the accordion in the corner, before looking up at my dad leaning against a pole. "Did you say it's about an hour away?"

He gave a short nod but didn't elaborate.

"Wow, you really hid this guy well. Right across the island."

"It was the best I could do," my dad admitted. "There is a natural well of magic near the Brooklyn Bridge. It serves as both a beacon and a camouflage to protect him."

It was weird to be able to talk to my dad again. This was my chance to finally ask my dad all the questions I'd been wanting to all these years. But now that I had an idea what he was, what he'd been doing, everything else seemed irrelevant. Still, what better way to fill the silent train ride?

I chewed on the insides of my cheeks. "So...what actually happened to you years ago?" I kept my voice low so only he could hear. "Did you really die?"

My dad met my gaze steadily. "In a way." He tilted his head in thought, straining to find the right words to explain. "I think Freyjn has shown you a magic technique called glamor? It's sort of like that."

I managed a nod. "What...actually *are* you?"

He narrowed his eyes ever so slightly, as though he needed to be more careful with his answers. "That's a little more of a complicated question right now."

"Really?" I quipped, wryly. "More complicated than if I ask why you decided to abandon your whole family? Why, in many of my childhood memories, my father was zoned out or altogether absent? You missed out on so many things, Dad. Good things. Bad things." I ran my fingers through my hair. "Sure, Mom, Erin, and I managed to deal with it eventually, but still..."

"You didn't need me. You still don't."

Muted, I shook my head. "I would have liked you around. Even if I didn't need you."

Remorse painted my dad's face. "But I was! I was just—" As if hesitating to continue his defense, he blew out a breath.

I caught a glimpse of the Brooklyn Bridge out the window and an odd memory struck me right then about a family trip to the park when I was younger.

It had been a big deal—celebrating a leadership award I'd received at school, and as usual, my father had not been in attendance. I'd always thought I was merely seeing things. But back then, I could have sworn I had spotted him around the area, speaking to some people...or—shoot, was he fighting with them?

I furrowed my eyebrows to strain to remember.

Oh, jeez. If I went back through all my miserable childhood memories, would I actually find the exact same thing? My absent father had been "absent," but it had been for one very particular, very important reason.

A heavy unease in my chest, I turned to study my dad's face. His eyes were sharp, narrowed, alert... But looking closer, they were also...tired, sad.

"Son, I am truly sorry I wasn't there for your childhood. Although I watched you all go through everything. I tried to help you, your mom, and your sister in every other way I was able to. I'll always regret missing out on our family life together." He braced one hand on my shoulder. "But now seeing the fine young man you've grown into, it already makes me prouder than I could be. And for that, I know I made the right decision."

Swallowing hard, I tamped down the well of emotion in my chest. Hell, if I was going to cry on the Brooklyn subway...

Taking a deep breath to reset myself, I cast a cautious glance over at Freyjn to make sure she hadn't noticed I was about to blubber like a big baby on the train.

My dad detected my gaze stray, his eyes narrowing to study my face again. "Oh, Josh..."

"What?" I asked, fully conscious my cheeks had turned beet red.

My dad just shook his head. "I know that look." His voice lowered just as mine had previously to keep our conversation between the two of us.

"What look?"

"What's the name of that girl—was it Mandy at your grade school prom? Quite a duplicitous little thing for an eleven-year-old if I remember correctly." He snapped his fingers a few times as if to jog his memory.

"Oh my god, Dad." Eyes widening, I shushed over his words, casting a furtive glance over to double-check that Freyjn still wasn't paying us any attention. "That was so many years ago. I can't believe you're bringing that up now."

"I'm just saying, you need to recognize situations where you need to step back," he chided. "I know you're strong, Josh. You've always been the kid who wants to see the best in any situation. But maybe in this case, you ought to actually stop and think about what's best for you, before you do any-thing you're going to regret."

I shot him a suspicious look. "That's odd. Mom and Erin are always pushing me to find a girlfriend."

Slightly aggravated, he rubbed his face with one hand. "Kid, you know what, I'm all for it. Live your best life. Settle down. Find a girl. Just—" He tilted his head in meaning, his voice a hoarse whisper. "Not that one."

Trying to process what he was saying, I pursed my lips.

So my dad wasn't specifically bothered about me and girls.

Unless the girl was Freyjn.

I supposed it was obvious why.

It was for the same reasons I'd been reminding myself all day yesterday and today.

He was right, of course.

Taking a deep breath, I shook off my long-buried melancholy from the past, as well as my hopeless fantasies of the future. I forced my brain to focus on the present. It might be futile, but all I could do was make the most of whatever time I had with her.

Coming off the subway, Freyjn and I trailed behind my dad as he strode down the uneven sidewalks of the city.

The path sloped down toward an old industrial area. Metallic clangs of dollies rolling over concrete, the hum of idling truck engines, and the occasional bark of orders cut through the damp, heavy air. Diesel fumes mixed with the salty aroma of the nearby docks, layered with the faint mustiness of cardboard and wooden pallets.

Tucked beneath the shadow of the Brooklyn Bridge, the loading bay pulsed with the quiet efficiency of workers in identical gray uniforms, moving in a seamless rhythm, blending into the machinery of the operation.

Pausing across the street, my dad surveyed the goings-on for a minute before declaring, "There he is."

Both Freyjn's and my gaze snapped toward the one guy who had visibly stepped closer to the open doors.

The guy looked about the same age as me. Tall, built, with sandy blond hair. wearing the same plain gray overalls as the rest of the people working busily behind him.

Biting my lip, I cast a discreet glance down at Freyjn. The look in her wide eyes made my heart pound.

Eager anticipation.

She'd finally found him.

The blond guy looked over. His eyes lit up, possibly because the three of us stuck out like a sore thumb amidst the industrial street block. But he raised his hand in greeting, his blue eyes crinkling at the corners.

"Hey, Bill!"

Eyebrows snapping together, I shot my dad a puzzled look.

But my dad waved back, "Hey, Damien," before gesturing for Freyjn and me to follow as he crossed the street.

A friendly grin on his face, Damien took off his gloves, brushing his shiny blond hair back from falling across his forehead. The movement stretched his sleeves taut over his obviously toned biceps.

I hated him already.

My dad glanced up and down the busy street and company operations. "There somewhere we can talk?"

"Oh, sure." Damien jumped. "Break room's over here." He pointed toward the offices lining the inside of the building. He waved to a couple of worker guys we walked past. "Just taking a break," he called.

Once he'd led us through the doors, Damien ambled to the kitchenette. "I didn't forget to pay this month's rent or something, did I?" he asked over his shoulder. He poured each of us a cup of coffee from the regular blend thermos.

Across from me standing at one of the tall tables, my dad gave me a look to explain. "I manage an apartment building here in the old industrial area."

"Bill is my landlord," Damien explained with a smile as he came over holding three Styrofoam cups in his hands.

My dad looked at Damien. "Nothing's wrong with the rent, kid. We just need your help with a little something."

"I see." Damien's easy smile was tinged with puzzlement. His eyes slid over to Freyjn who had gone to stand and gaze out the window which looked out to the busy working floor. "What can I do you all for today?"

I didn't miss Damien checking her out, his gaze lingering on the back of her colorful dress. Though not in a sleazy way, just in appreciation.

I couldn't fight the urge to walk over to her. I shrugged my jacket off and draped it over her again like last night. I let my hands settle on Freyjn's shoulders for a moment even as she turned to meet Damien's gaze.

"Well..." My dad cleared his throat. Casting a glance to make sure none of the other workers were anywhere near us, his eyebrows rose as he gave Freyjn an expectant prompting look.

Freyjn didn't seem at all daunted in the slightest. Her chin was tilted up as if in authority. "I need to see if you have a mark on your chest. Could you?" She gestured for him to undo the buttons on his overalls.

It seemed she didn't need to ask him twice.

Damien followed her instructions with a nod.

I shifted in my stance when Freyjn came up closer to inspect him.

His face drawn taut, my dad's shoulders were tense as Damien tugged the top of his overalls open.

I'd already seen Freyjn and my dad do different kinds of magic over the last few days, but the mystical golden swirling mark on Damien's chest was completely otherworldly.

I almost held my breath. "Whoa..."

A bright glowing sphere overlain a shimmering serpentine creature spewing out a violent flare of potent fire right hovered about an inch or so from the middle of his freakishly well-defined chest.

Freyjn's eyes were wide. That smoky purple glow manifested all over her, accompanied by the irrational wind swirling around in the room. "Curse Bearer." She broke a soft smile. "You shall awaken the sleeping magic across the realm of Arcadia and save my world."

"What..." Damien's eyes were wide as well.

I could only imagine Damien's brain was probably trying to make heads or tails of what he was seeing, but failing miserably.

A corner of my mouth tilted up in a knowing smirk.

You got that right, dude. Magic does exist.

Damien's face paled so fast.

None of us was prepared for what happened next—except Freyjn.

When Mr. Pretty Boy threw up, Freyjn was able to summon a quick sparkly shield to protect herself from the spray.

Just herself.

17

Chapter Seventeen - Sacrifice

My dad had been behind Damien so he had avoided the Mum...upchuck.

Grumbling in annoyance, I shook my head as he led Mr. Pretty Boy to slump in a chair across the room. Cup of water in hand, my dad seemed to be managing to talk Damien down, even as his eyes darted up and around to make sure nobody else had glimpsed all the traces of magic that had overwhelmed the little breakroom.

"Found this." Freyjn thrust a clean, threadbare shirt at me as I stood by the sink with a washcloth.

"Thanks." I heaved a sigh. I'd already washed my face. Cringing, I slipped my ruined shirt up over my head. If I didn't breathe in through my nose, I almost didn't smell the putrid stench.

This was great. *Juuust gr—*

Freyjn picked up the damp washcloth and dabbed at the side of my neck.

I sucked in a half-startled breath, stiffening like a board.

Tilting her head, she wiped the top of my shoulder, my collarbone.

Instead of keeping far away from what I was entirely sure was a revolting sight *and* smell, Freyjn was helping me clean up. She was standing so close, I was sure if I bent my head, her fragrant hair would brush against my forehead.

Ohh... There was a keening hum in my head. She could probably hear my skin practically thrumming at the thrill. She had to stop touching me. I had to stop her.

Somehow, my voice came out all low and rumbly. "You don't have to do that."

Those brilliant, violet eyes looked up to meet my gaze for a moment before dropping back to my bare chest.

Without warning, she stepped away. "Okay," she said, her tone short, offhand.

Heart pounding, I almost teetered off-balance.

Holy crap, Josh. Snap out of it.

Was she provoking me on purpose? Did she even realize what she was doing to me?

Freyjn turned to walk across the room toward my dad and Damien and a hollow formed in my stomach. Struck with a seriously strange feeling, I looked down at my chest again.

Wait, did I suddenly feel jealous of Damien? Because he had the mark and I didn't? Because I wasn't the one she was looking for?

I immediately halted that train of thought.

Blowing out another annoyed sigh at myself, I pulled the clean shirt on.

I should be relieved and grateful that Freyjn had completed her mission.

She could go back to her world and I would...never see her again.

His voice rising from their likely previously quiet conversation, my dad was even crankier than before. "Yes, yes, fine."

Poor Damien was slumped in the chair, his gaze still distant. He'd clearly had no idea who he really was or what was going on. He was probably resisting the urge to smack himself awake from this vivid hallucination.

Waving his hand, my dad gave Freyjn a flat look. "Now you've seen him. Mission complete."

Freyjn nodded. "Yes, and now I need to take him back to my realm."

"No." My dad shook his head pointedly, matter-of-factly. "I'm afraid I can't let you do that. You can ask him all the questions you like or divine any sort of magic but he stays here."

She gawked at him. "What? But this was the whole point of my quest. I must take him back."

His eyebrows furrowed. "It's too risky. What if he doesn't survive?"

Freyjn put her hands on her hips in haughty dismissal. "He is a being of two worlds. Of course, he will survive. His destiny is among my people."

"But he has a life here, on Earth," my dad protested. "A family. Friends."

Freyjn's eyes were bright in steely resolution. "That is all secondary. He is the savior of my realm. Without him, all is lost. Everything I'll have done up to this point will have been in vain."

My dad's face crumpled like he knew he was struggling to swim upstream but still determined to try. "Is there truly no other way?"

"Not that I am aware."

"But are you sure you've tried everything? Perhaps there is a way your people simply haven't discovered yet."

Freyjn's head tipped to one side, her eyes narrowed. "Why are you so adamantly fighting this? Do you know of the prophecy as well?"

My dad stiffened. His gaze drifted to meet mine but only for a moment. "Only the highlights."

"Then you know I have no choice in this." Freyjn's chin tipped up once again. "We must return to my realm now."

Sighing, my dad rubbed the back of his neck. "If I can't stop you..." he trailed off in resignation.

I looked from the dejected expression on my dad's face to the authoritative, almost threatening one on Freyjn's.

"You cannot."

I pursed my lips. *Yep.* There was no saying 'no' to that face.

My dad tried to help Damien get up, but the 'Curse Bearer' swayed in his stance. As if he didn't trust his own legs to keep himself upright. His gaze was downcast, his shoulders slumped completely.

This time, I felt sorry for him.

Sighing again, my dad gestured to the door. "Let me at least clock the poor kid out," he said before exiting the room.

I blew out a sigh too. Carefully stepping over the splatter of throw-up mess on the floor, I walked toward the closet labeled 'Cleaning' to find the mop. There wasn't much to deal with. Lucky for him (though unlucky for me), it seemed I had caught the most of the...damage.

Damien finally lifted his head. "Oh please, I can't let you do that."

I put my hand up. "I clean up messes for a living. Don't worry about it."

Freyjn was standing by the window again, arms crossed over her chest, my leather jacket still around her shoulders.

Damien glanced at her before looking back at me. "Are you magic too?"

"Me?" I scoffed. "No. I was just accidentally recruited to help find you."

"So...she's magic." Damien looked up at Freyjn. "And Bill...?"

I shrugged. "I suppose, yes."

"Am I going somewhere?"

Freyjn met my gaze for a moment and her chin clenched. She probably wasn't eager to have to explain everything all over again.

Besides that, somehow, I felt the explanation might sound a lot less threatening coming from me. That was, if we didn't want Damien to throw up at the shock a second time.

I gestured to Freyjn. "You're going with her. She has to bring you to her realm through a portal doorway of sorts. And hey, you get to save the world. Doesn't that sound cool?"

"Cool..." he echoed flatly without indication of agreement.

"Hey, you didn't want to haul boxes on pallets for the rest of your life, did you?" I chided lightly. "Maybe there's something better for you out there."

"Maybe." Damien sighed. "I'd always wanted to move out west. A friend of mine started his own shipping business in California. Seemed interesting. But I'd always felt something compelling me to stay here."

I grimaced in sympathy. I wondered if my dad's magic had contributed to that urge.

When I finished mopping up, I put the cleaning supplies away. "Maybe you can call your family and tell them you're going on a long vacation or something."

Damien shook his head. "My parents died when I was young. I'm an only child."

My eyebrows furrowed in curious puzzlement.

Before I could dig deeper, my dad rapped on the open door. He didn't bother coming back in. "I logged Damien out as sick," he relayed, "which I'm sure nobody will dispute given the smell in here." He waved his hand for us to come out.

I helped Damien to his feet. He seemed a lot less woozy now that he'd had a few minutes to absorb his situation.

"What happens now?" I was the one to ask once we were out of the delivery bay.

"I assume you need to find a secluded area to summon your portal?" my dad prompted Freyjn, even as it seemed he was already leading the way. "We're right by the park."

Freyjn stepped past me to walk ahead. "Good."

Shoving my hands in my pockets, I lagged behind the three of them, behind Damien, sort of to make sure he didn't pass out or anything.

I chewed on the insides of my cheek in deep thought.

Was I still jealous of him? What would I actually do if it was me that had to be called away to another realm? I would have to leave my family, my friends, my job—oh right, I didn't have a job anymore. At least, that was an easy choice.

I blew out an aggravated breath. I couldn't even hold on to a proper job. I couldn't make anything work. Did I even belong anywhere? Was everything I'd ever done completely pointless? What was I really doing with my life?

Glancing up at the others, the weight on my chest only pressed harder. My dad's goals were clear. Freyjn had a one-track mind on her mission right from the start. Damien just found his purpose.

After all this, *I* was going to go back to my normal day-to-day.

With nothing.

My gaze lingered on Freyjn.

Less than nothing.

Crossing the street, my dad glanced over his shoulder. "Can the kid have a last meal at least? It's lunchtime and I know a hotdog cart vendor over there in the park who owes me a favor."

"Fine." Freyjn let out a long sigh. But then she called out quickly, "Please fetch me some sandwiches as well."

I thought my dad was going to shake his head in amusement, but he merely cracked a smirk. "Sure." He gestured ahead. "This path leads to the waterfront. You can follow it down, take Damien with you first. There's some picnic tables, some benches. Josh and I will go pick up the hotdogs."

Freyjn gave a curt nod. She curled a finger to beckon Damien over. "This way."

He didn't protest.

Curious, I tilted my head as I watched the pair of them walk off down the pavement. "Funny how she can order him around so easy."

My dad shrugged. "That's part of her magic. Most humans will do anything she says."

I frowned again. An uneasy stir rattled in my brain. Droplets in a bucket of truth. A grain of sand on the shore of knowledge. A crumb in a cookie jar of clues. But much like the persistent fog in my dreams, I couldn't quite grasp the whole of it before they were swept away.

I caught up to my dad as he quickly walked ahead. "It's kind of nice of you to look out for Damien."

He cleared his throat. "It's my job."

"Being his landlord?" I noted, still somewhat puzzled.

"Among other things."

"It's also funny. There's a different hotdog guy who owes me a favor too from—oh, shoot, right." I stopped to turn back. "Freyjn's wearing my jacket, my wallet—"

"No! Josh, wait—"

The urgent alarm in my dad's tone should have tripped me up, but I was already sprinting back across the park.

Peering past the bushes as I came around the corner, I almost skidded to a stop.

Half a dozen of those menacing warrior dudes had encircled one of the benches close to the waterfront railing—right where Freyjn and Damien were.

Uh-oh.

The warriors were probably disguised as college bullies again or perhaps innocent tourists as far as anyone else but I could see.

Freyjn was about to do something with her hands when two of them grabbed her arms from behind. A bright spark of light flashed and Damien collapsed to the ground.

Alarmed, my eyes widened and I ran faster.

"No!" I thought I heard Freyjn yell.

"Hey—!" I called out.

Freyjn's gaze whipped over to meet mine—right before another warrior popped up directly on the path in front of me.

I was running too fast to stop. I smacked face first straight into his meaty chest.

And everything went dark.

18

Chapter Eighteen - Captured

Saltwater mixed with the sour tang of rust and damp wood tickled my nose.

My head throbbed as I blinked awake.

The scant light from sunset streaked in through the small windows of the storage shed, hydraulic pump control shed, or whatever place this was.

Thick ropes bit into my wrists, binding them behind my back, and tied them down to a metal pipe embedded through the grimy concrete floor. My shoulders ached as if I'd been like this for a few hours.

"Finally."

My pulse jumped at the familiar exasperated sigh carrying a hint of annoyance that was unmistakeably Freyjn. I turned my head, spotting my fairy sitting on a wooden rocking chair across the room. I gave her an urgent once-over, before sighing in relief that she appeared unharmed. I still asked, "Are you okay?"

She made an effort to shift in her seat to show me her arms were tied behind her too, one wrist braced to each side of the back of her chair.

The muted ferry foghorn groaning through the walls, accompanied by faint strains of carnival music, signaled that we were still in the vicinity of the docks.

"We must be near the park carousel," I guessed, looking around the dank space.

"Where's Damien?" Freyjn's tone was alarmed, if her wide eyes didn't already give that away.

I tipped my head to one side. Freyjn couldn't see that Damien was curled up in a heap right behind her. "He's there. He's tied up too." Cold dread threatened to spread within me. "He's not moving..."

"No! Is he dead?" she cried out.

I squinted to see in the dim light. Noting the steady rise and fall of his breathing, I shook my head. "No. Probably just passed out."

With a huge relieved sigh, she slumped back in her seat.

As the realization dawned on me, I cringed at the stabbing in my chest. "My dad... He set us up. I can't believe this."

Freyjn met my gaze, hers was soft as if in sympathy.

My heart sank in my stomach. I hung my head, squeezing my eyes shut for a moment.

How on earth did I let this happen? My dad was a bad guy?

Then again, he'd been gone for years—abandoned his family for years. How was I really supposed to know who he was, what he was...?

I should have asked more questions, insisted on more answers, not just assumed he was intrinsically virtuous underneath it all. And I definitely wanted to kick myself in the head for even beginning to trust him again. I supposed after everything, much like any son, I still wanted to think of my dad as my hero.

This was all my fault. What even was wrong with me? His entire history with my family should have been proof enough.

I should have known.

Still, there was a fresh ache in my chest.

What was that my dad told me on the subway? I was the kind of person who always wanted to see the best in any situation.

Served me right.

Giving myself a brisk shake to push those thoughts away, I straightened in my seat. Right now, it was better that I focused instead on things I could control. Sucking my cheeks in, I tested the ropes restraining my hands.

Freyjn was still casting me a wary look. She tilted her chin over her shoulder, as though in reference to the unconscious human heap behind her. "Technically, your father set *us* up. Not you."

The way she phrased it bothered me, but I was determined to put my grievances with my dad aside. I turned my thoughts to something else. "Why are you still here? I thought these warrior guys wanted to take you home any-way. You've already found Damien. You all can totally go now."

She bit her lip. "It's not that simple."

I shot her a confused look.

Her eyes were wide in alarm once again. "I'm afraid they might kill Damien."

"What? Why?" I asked, aghast.

"Some of my people will stop at nothing to disprove what I believe," she implored in earnest. "That the 'Curse Bearer' *will* save my world. Without Damien, I won't have any proof whatsoever." She dropped her gaze. "And they won't want to risk me trying to come back here and retrieving him again. I'm sure I've given them enough trouble this time around. Freyjn—" She stopped short as if stunned.

I blinked. "What?"

Her shoulders stiffened quickly, the hesitation in her tone cleared up. "The point is...I have to save him. I have to complete my mission. *They* won't help me." Her face crum-pled in annoyed displeasure. "I mean, the warriors definitely don't intend to hurt me, but...I'm pretty sure they don't like me very much either."

Freyjn wore such an uneasy look of irritable distaste. De-spite the situation, I couldn't help a smirk. "Oh, gee. I won-der why."

Seriously, I'd only known her a couple of days, and I could already swear I understood exactly why her guess might be entirely true.

Glaring at me, she pursed her lips—but there was mirth in those sparkling eyes. She was...holding back a chuckle. "Stop making jokes at times like this."

"But you're laughing," I pointed out.

She shook her head, the look in her eyes softening again, short of rolling her eyes in disbelief. As if realizing that I would never take things too seriously, but also maybe realizing she was starting to appreciate it as well.

"Sorry," I mumbled anyway. "So then, what are these goons waiting for? Shouldn't they have like killed Damien already and whisked you back to your realm?"

Freyjn's tone was somber as she explained. "These warriors are not natural portal wielders. To bring all of us back to my realm, including their entire horde, they need the amplified magical resonance emanated by the bridge." She cast a glance out the small window as if to check the time of day. "It only comes at dusk. Soon..."

My dad (the traitor) did say there was a natural well of magic around the Brooklyn Bridge.

I leaned forward in my seat. "What do you need to do?"

"Well, I need to get the hell out of here first before they all come back," she declared, her eyes shining eagerly. "That way, I can summon my own portal so Damien and I can escape."

Damien and I...

I tried not to let the sharp twinge in my chest affect my expression. Nodding slowly, my brain went into immediate strategizing. It was clear what I had to do now. I needed to help Freyjn escape so she could take Damien and portal back to her realm.

She wriggled her hands behind her in full exasperation. "I can't call on my magic because of the way they've tied my hands, but..." she trailed off, her eyes widening yet again.

Because I moved to brace one palm against the floor to push myself up, warily testing my shaky legs.

"Are you—what?" Her eyebrows snapped together. "How did you get out of your binds?

I shrugged, tugging on what was left of the rope around my wrist before it dropped to the ground. "I'm really good with knots."

She gestured to the bind on her hands. "Untie me, quickly."

"Yeah, yeah, I *was* gonna do that." I shook my head at her impatience as I walked over. I crouched beside her to untie the ropes fastening her to the chair.

Once she was unbound, I caught her elbow to help her straighten up.

Before I could say anything, Freyjn grabbed my arm and the words rushed out of her mouth. "Josh, I release you from your oath."

"What?" I felt an instant alleviation, as though a heavy weight on my chest disintegrated to float off into the ether.

"I have completed my mission," she implored, wide-eyed. "I have what I came for. You no longer have to help me. Now, run away! Get as far as you can from this place before you get hurt too."

There was a thud of disappointment in my stomach, of a different nature. Indignant protest burned in my chest. "What? No."

"What do you mean 'no'?" she mocked.

I gritted my teeth. "I told you already I'm not leaving you."

"Ugh!" Groaning, she closed her eyes for a moment in frustration. "You are incorrigible!"

"That's me. Josh, The Incorrigible."

"Why?" She threw up her hands. "Why are you even doing this?"

I met her gaze in silence.

I had an answer, but it wasn't one that made any sense.

I put my hand up. "Look, can you just—I want to make sure you get away safely first," I insisted. It wasn't like I had any other semblance of purpose anyway. I might as well help with hers. "What if something else goes wrong?" I dropped my gaze for a moment. "I want to stay here...just in case you still need me."

There were too many emotions in Freyjn's eyes for a change. I couldn't read them. Rolling her eyes, she blew out a breath. "Fine. Have it your way."

Walking around the rocking chair to stand beside the crumpled heap that was Damien, Freyjn braced her feet apart, clasping her hands together in preparation for summoning her portal. "This is seriously silly." She gave me a flat, pointed look. "And ridiculous." She spread her fingers, pulling her palms slowly apart. "And reckless. And—don't blame me if the moment we're gone, those goons storm in here and throw you around a little."

"Just do it already." I folded my arms across my chest, preparing myself for the sight of that brilliant swirling portal once again.

Freyjn visibly swallowed, her eyes clouding over. "I thought I already did." Her shoulders tensed once again. "What...?"

"What?" I looked around similarly at a loss. "Was something supposed to happen?"

She cursed under her breath, her gaze scanning the room. "They must have put wards on this shed." She squinted in frustration. "It's too dark. I can't see where the wards could be. They could be hidden anywhere. I won't be able to summon in here." She buried her face in one hand and groaned. "Aghh—dammit! I have to bring Damien outside a sufficient distance away first before I can use magic."

"Huh," I huffed, somewhat impressed as that struck me as a bit of a surprise. It appeared those menacing warriors weren't simply mindless blockheads either, if they'd planned for this contingency.

When Freyjn's suffering gaze slid back to meet mine, I was already tamping down my I-told-you-so grin.

"Can you just help me drag this heavy heap outside, please?" she grumbled past clenched teeth.

My self-satisfied smile widened. "As you wish."

19

Chapter Nineteen - Last Chance

Emerging from the musty shed, my nose twitched at the whiff of the East River. The odd humidity crawled along my skin before I pulled my leather jacket back on.

Freyjn cast a furtive glance around the area, but it was quiet. Those menacing warriors weren't hiding out in the shadows of dusk to ambush us in the middle of the park. Either that or they were hiding themselves really well.

Satisfied with her check, she signaled me to move.

Still passed out, Damien's one arm was slung across her shoulders, his other across mine as we awkwardly carried him along the grassy lawn.

"I see it." Freyjn pointed across the beach. "There, magic hums once more."

I looked up to nod then stopped short. "Whoa. That's so weird," I noted in marvel. "They've put on some fancy giant lights to illuminate the bridge tonight. I wonder what the occasion is. The whole thing even looks like it's glowing."

Freyjn shot me an incredulous look. She was so stunned it took a few seconds before she managed to pointedly reply, "Those...aren't fancy giant lights." Forehead creased, she tilted her head in bewilderment. "How...how can *you* see the magical aura of the bridge?"

My eyes bulged. "Is that what I'm seeing?" I cast my gaze back up at the majestic Brooklyn Bridge, glimmering against the sparkling river and cityscape. "I don't know. I thought that your magic was letting me see things I normally shouldn't." I stopped short. "But wait, didn't you just...?"

Her tone was matter-of-fact. "Yeah-huh. I just released you from that oath. Like literally minutes ago."

"Hmm... Maybe there's a lag?" I proposed.

"Huh." Freyjn didn't look convinced, but she didn't press the matter.

Who possibly knew how her weird oath magic worked anyhow? I certainly knew less than nothing about magic. Regular, weak human boy that I was.

Under the glow of the bridge, the gravel crunched beneath my sneakers as we half-dragged, half-carried Damien across the beach. The stones shifted treacherously at our feet as the tide sloshed against the shoreline, whispering over the rocks like something lurking just out of sight.

It must have been from all the jostling, but Damien stirred, if only for a moment. "What...?" His eyelids fluttered as he lifted his head before it dropped once again.

I whistled. "Man, Damien is really out of it." Grunting, I adjusted my hold on him, bracing my arm about his torso to keep him upright, before glancing around.

Freyjn noticed my gaze wander. "What are you looking for?"

"Scrap metal or cardboard or something. Maybe we can make a flatbed cart or stretcher for him to make this easier."

Freyjn pursed her lips. "You really are quite resourceful. I guess you must indeed be more like your father than you realize."

Tamping down a bolt of anger, I bit out, "I'm nothing like him! He set you up. I would *never* do that to you."

Her eyes widened at my outburst.

I immediately regretted snapping at her. I closed my eyes for a moment. "I'm-I'm sorry. That anger wasn't directed at you."

When Freyjn's eyes met mine again, hers was soft. "Look...you can leave now if you want. Just run away. I can carry Damien from here."

"You can?" I grimaced. "Then...why did I have to help you?"

She shot me a cross between a cringe and an eye roll. "I mean, I *can* carry him. I just...didn't want to." Her response was all kinds of haughty.

I bit my lip in almost mirth. She was adorable when she was trying to look tough. "Never mind. We're almost there anyway."

The looming bridge's glow cast a fractured shimmer across the water. As we reached the paved boardwalk, Freyjn assessed the crowd with a pensive frown.

The dusky sky stretched wide over the river, painted in swirling hues of pinks and purples as the last remnants of daylight melted into the encroaching night. With the fine weather, there was no lack of innocent passers-by milling around the park.

Freyjn's tone was as ominous as ever. "Be on the lookout. I know those warriors are here somewhere. If they saw it fit to ward the shed against magic, they must also already know we've escaped."

I followed her gaze to double-check. "I only see tourists."

A young couple, sharing a cloud of cotton candy, strolling along the boardwalk past us tracked our little trio in suspicion, eyeing Damien's unconscious form slung between the two of us.

I flashed them a big grin, calling out, "Oh, he's just had one too many. Friday nights, you know how it is."

Luckily, they turned back to mind their own business.

The brilliant glass shell of the restored vintage park carousel up ahead provided a stark contrast to the iconic bridge set against the backdrop of Manhattan. Encasing the brightly-colored circle of delicate horses in mid-gallop, it glittered under its own lights while children's merry laughter tinkled amidst the early evening, the air carrying hints of sugary cotton with it.

The view was so picturesque and serene.

Too serene.

Cold dread was already working its way from my stomach to the rest of my body. No way was this going to be this easy.

As if on cue, the carousel lights snapped off with a sharp mechanical click, and stifled cries and gasps overwhelmed the crowd at the pavilion.

Darkness swallowed the area, leaving only the faint glimmer of the carousel housing, reflecting the faraway lights of the urban cityscape.

It seemed a mere trick of light at first, a flicker, a ripple in the huge glass panels, a shady haze stretching the wrong way beneath a lamppost.

Until they began to move.

Figures peeled away from the glass, forms warping as if stepping through liquid, bodies solidifying with each unnatural stride. Park branches cast shadows that slithered into men, mirrored surfaces birthing pursuers from nothing, silhouettes among the crowd of harmless bystanders unfolded into the same menacing warriors.

One shadow broke away from the rest, striding toward the glass, the faint glow of the city illuminating a glint of steel at its side. A second figure followed. Then a third. Then more. Then even more.

Oh, shoot.

That cold dread quickly transformed into nausea.

How many of these freaking magical warriors were in Brooklyn right now?

Alarmed, I looked around. Of course, as far as everyone else on the boardwalk was concerned, it was just a good old regular temporary power cut.

But I could still see them. Despite Freyjn having terminated that magical binding oath, I could still see the horde of grim-faced, leather-and-polished-steel-uniformed goons as they emerged from nearly every surface.

My pulse hammering against my ribs, I cast a glance at Freyjn.

She exhaled slowly, flexing her fingers.

I checked on Damien again. He was still totally out of it. Could we possibly make a break for it while at the same time carrying his unconscious slump to safety? I swallowed hard. "Um, now what?"

I could tell she was trying not to show the panic on her face. She knew as well as I did, our chances of evading capture were slim to none.

Clenching her jaw in bull-headed determination anyway, Freyjn flicked a glance toward the bridge. So close. "We're almost there. We need to run."

Following her lead, we took off as fast as we could, but Damien's dead weight slowed us way down. Each step was a battle against exhaustion, against inevitability. For a split second, the world lurched and Damien's weight slipped from our grasp.

"Damn it—" Freyjn muttered as she as I grabbed him under the shoulders, scrambling to lift his legs to heave him up.

My muscles burning, I pushed through the ache and continued staggering forward.

We cut past a cluster of picnic tables, ducking past statues, and sculptures, but the menacing warriors were coordinated, efficient.

When we turned left, they were there. When we turned right, they were there.

They were herding us.

Hissing under my breath, I shot Freyjn a look. "For the record, you wouldn't have made it this far without me."

Her eyes incredulous, her protest was indignant. "I would have if I had magic."

"Well, you don't."

"Are you seriously trying to be funny again right now?"

"Why can't you just admit you need me?" I couldn't help but tease, if only to distract my nerves through our imminently perilous situation.

"Shut up, Josh!"

By the time we reached the grassy knoll directly beneath the glowing bridge, Freyjn's triumphant declaration was breathless, "We're going to make it."

Except when we skidded to a stop, the warriors were right on top of us.

Or not. I gulped between pants as my eyes tracked each foreboding figure closing in.

We were surrounded.

Chapter Twenty - Reveal

Up close, the warriors looked almost human—but not quite. Many donned long flowing hair, had pointy ears, their skin an unusual hue. Quite a few of them were even very noticeably square-jawed with fine features, possibly even attractive—terribly so, but at the moment, their eyes were dark voids.

They most definitely had not come in peace.

I mumbled sideways at Freyjn. "So...seventy-ish against two, how do those odds sound to you?"

Her wide eyes met mine. The steely determination was still solid in that violet gaze. She wasn't going to give up. She was going to fight to the end.

Before she could say anything, a shadow dropped from the massive steel beams above. For a split second, it seemed like he would crash into the ground, a broken body among the grass. But then—he landed right beside us, feet braced apart steadily, the tail of his trench coat flying wild behind him with the odd swirl of wind.

My eyes very nearly popped out of my head. "Dad!"

My outcry was punctuated by a crackle and searing light as my dad raised his hands to instantly summon a bright spherical shield encompassing our little group.

As if set off by his arrival, all seventy-ish of the menacing warriors aimed steady blasts of magic right at us in an attempt to take down the shield. But the shield's defense merely split the night with deafening whip-like sizzles as magic ricocheted and hissed all around us.

Staring at my dad's back, my mind spun. Every emotion rushed through my body like a fresh torrent of renewed confusion.

Was he here to save us or was he simply here to trap us again?

My dad had basically delivered Freyjn and Damien to the warriors on a silver platter before. He had abandoned me and my entire family for years.

I was already resolved to think of him as a bad guy, but...

Damn me and my seeing the best in any situation.

My dad straightened, looking at us over his shoulder. "I thought you could use some help."

The spherical shield solidified around us. With the onslaught of the other streams of powerful magic attacking us from outside, the view of the cityscape became a mere golden haze, the noise muting into a low roar. It was a welcome reprieve—if however temporary.

With a distrustful glare, Freyjn shifted to set Damien down on the ground within our little circle of protection. "How dare you show your face here again? How could you possibly believe I would accept anything from you, let alone your help?"

Both hands still raised to maintain the shield around us, my dad grunted softly. He didn't respond to Freyjn. He was looking at me, waiting for me to meet his gaze.

Crouched beside Damien, I confirmed he was settled first. When I finally looked at my dad, he almost winced at the muted fury and disappointment I was sure was all over my face right then. I clenched my teeth, my question almost too quiet. "How could you do that to them? You sold them out to the bad guys. After everything you've done, I wanted to give you another chance and you blew it. Why, Dad?"

My dad's face was agonized, frustrated. "Because! You should know by now, son, I would do anything to keep you safe."

Straightening back up, I glared at him. "What makes you think we're going to trust anything you say right now?"

He sighed. "Because now, I'm actually going to tell you the truth." He shook his head, glancing over at Freyjn for a moment. "You cannot take Damien to the other realm."

I burst out in annoyance, "You just said—"

Freyjn's eyes were wide as if she'd already figured it out.

I supposed I was too much in emotional turmoil, it took me a second.

My dad gave me a pointed look. "He is not the true 'Curse Bearer.'"

Then, somehow—*somehow*, it clicked almost immediately.

I sucked in my breath.

No. Freaking. Way.

"Damien was unfortunately merely someone I used as a decoy," my dad relayed. "In case anyone from her realm came looking. I made sure I'd picked someone who had no other connections to this world, just in case. But since then, I also made sure he still lived a good life."

I was frozen where I stood.

My dad's head shake was rueful. "Josh, your 'breakdown' from years ago was no breakdown at all. A magical being from the other realm had managed to summon you through, trying to kill you. Luckily, you made it back here somehow. And when you did, I had to erase your memories of the other world."

He winced with a grunt, adjusting his hands to reinforce his magic. No doubt the warriors were pummelling his shield nonstop from the outside.

"It's you, my son. You are the 'Curse Bearer'." His eyes were sad as he went on. "I'd set up many a misdirection and so many traps to keep you safe. I've been trying to protect you, to hide you in this world. To keep you away from hers." Sighing, he dropped his gaze. "That's why I didn't sense Freyjn's arrival. She was masked by the magical block I'd put on you."

My eyes widened.

It must have been true. The warriors didn't even detect us at all until Freyjn used her ice magic at the Ferris wheel.

Freyjn's remark was soft in realization. "No wonder my oath magic is weaker on you. Regular humans are much more easily swayed to do my bidding."

I blinked, recalling how much more easily she was able to order Damien around. I also recalled our first encounter, as indeed, she did seem surprised that I wouldn't follow her instructions or obey her whims off the bat. When she'd asked for food at my apartment that first time, she *had* expected that I would hop like a bunny to prepare it for her.

My heart pounded in my ears again.

It was me.

It was me all along.

My dad groaned again at the strain of maintaining the magical shield—its translucence flickering several times. "Watching you more closely last night, and all of today, I realized I've been underestimating you. You are more clever and braver than I'd let myself believe. You've taken all this life-changing information in stride without even losing your composure. You managed to wrangle—her." His gaze darted to Freyjn for a split second.

He let out a sigh. "I understand now, there is no stopping your fate, and you are more than capable enough to deal with it. You must go to the other world. You must let Freyjn take you there. You are destined to help her people, her realm."

Holy. Freaking. Shoot.

My mind whirled with confusion, dread, worry...

Freyjn had more urgent things on her mind. "We must get out of here immediately. Can you remove the block you put on your son?"

"All you need to do is channel your magic through him, and not only will he act as a magical amplifier, but this will also undo the blocking spell." My dad gave her a nod, before he hissed in pain, crumpling down to his knees.

"Dad!" I jumped to his side.

His eyes squeezed closed, his words a groan even as he struggled to keep both hands raised. "I won't be able to hold up the shield much longer. Make sure you are ready." I wasn't sure if he was talking to me or to Freyjn.

My chest ached. *Dad...* His skin was turning sallow as if the magic was draining all of his energy. He was giving everything he had to the shield protecting us—protecting me. What could I do? I didn't know what to do.

Freyjn's voice rang clear. "I know what to do."

My gaze snapped up to meet hers.

Her chin lifted in that usual authority. "Using the bridge magic and yours as an amplifier, I should be able to summon a portal big enough to dispel all of the warriors and send them back to my realm all at once." Those violet eyes settling on me, she crooked a finger to beckon me closer. "I need you."

Swallowing hard, I glanced down at my dad again.

He looked like he was about to pass out. But even with his eyes still closed, he chucked his chin to motion me away. "Go."

Taking a deep breath, I pushed to straighten up again and approached Freyjn. "What do you need me to do?"

I chewed the insides of my cheeks. I didn't want to be nervous, but I had no idea what it meant to 'unblock' me. Was it going to hurt? Was I going to lose my memories of the last two days all over again? Maybe longer?

"Put your arms around me."

I stopped at Freyjn's command. *What?*

My dad's shield noticeably flickered yet again, accompanied by his low groan.

Too impatient to wait for me to unfreeze, Freyjn yanked on my shirt until I stood flush against her back. Then she drew my arms up at either side, her hands around mine to hold them outstretched in front of us.

That fragrant hair was in my nose, her body warm against my chest. Another inkling of a memory tugged in the back of my mind. Why did everything with her always seem so very familiar?

My dad let out a loud cry before he finally collapsed in exhaustion and the spherical shield around us disappeared with a blink.

But Freyjn was ready.

She directed her magic into her hands, my hands, our hands...and another bright sphere formed around us—this time a shield summoned by Freyjn.

Purple smoke emanated from her body, and the wind blew fiercely in response, as a surge of compelling energy shot right through her, right through *me*.

A fresh searing sensation spread throughout my insides. It was similar to the stinging from yesterday when I tried to resist the binding oath but much more intense.

Much, much more intense.

"Aahh—" I gasped at the burn, trying to blink through the pain.

Freyjn's body jerked against my chest and I tightened my arms around her. Was she going to pass out too like my dad? Was all this too much for her as well?

I peered at her face in worry.

Her forehead creased in concentration but the corners of her mouth were turned up instead.

Breathless, I spoke low in her ear. "What is it?"

Turning sideways to meet my gaze, she studied my eyes as if in confirmed triumph, in pure satisfaction. "Your eyes," she noted. "I can see fire in them. I thought I saw it earlier too, at the party. But it's true. You are the 'Curse Bearer'."

At her words, another surge of warmth coursed through me.

A brilliant light burst above us—like the symbol from Damien's chest from before.

But it was *mine*.

The golden swirl was bigger, the glowing sphere even brighter, the shimmering dragon mark spewing out a potent fire so violent, it almost looked like it was spouting real flames as it lit up the sky right above our heads, swallowing us in its glow.

Turning her head to face front once again, Freyjn took a deep breath, murmured something, and thrust our hands forward.

The impact cracked through the air, sending a shockwave of energy that rippled outward like a breaking tide. The pavement shuddered. The wind roared. And from the ground beneath us, a burst of pulsing, translucent energy erupted, a shimmering dome of force that blasted—opening up to the massive mouth of an ethereal silvery-blue sphere bursting to life right above the East River.

Portal!

Freyjn shifted our hands ever so slightly.

Whatever she did, each and every one of those seventy-ish menacing warriors surrounding us was shunted off their feet, as though a rug had been pulled out from beneath them. Muffled yells and yelps punched the air as their bodies were sucked backward into the whorl of an eerie swirl hovering above the water.

"Oh, shoot," Freyjn cursed.

"What?" I startled.

"Too much—" Instead of finishing her explanation, she whirled around to bury her face in my chest.

Before I could even furrow my eyebrows in puzzlement, I looked up to see the mouth of the giant swirling vortex of doom warp and pulse, rumbling as it stretched out—

Uh-oh. It was going to—

With a blinding flash, the portal imploded, then detonated, sending a shockwave of raw force that rippled through the air, bending trees, tearing banners from poles, whirling leaves, and skidding benches across the ground with a metallic crash.

The river itself churned violently, waves slamming against the rocks as if recoiling from the unnatural force. For a breathless moment, the steel beams on the bridge above us even seemed to groan, their rivets trembling from the aftershock before the energy finally dissipated...

The lights on the carousel clicked back on, as the carnival music resumed.

Just another fine evening at the Brooklyn Bridge Park.

21

Chapter Twenty-One - The Break

Groaning, I opened my eyes.

The damp grass beneath my head tickled my ear as I lay flat on my back.

That portal implosion had blown nearly everything away. It was a good thing we were far enough from the crowd at the carousel, the shelter of the towering bridge obscuring most of the evidence of what had just happened, especially with the shadows of the night having fallen completely.

Fresh cut grass scent mingled with cypress and jasmine.

Freyjn was lying on my chest, my arms still tight around her, her wild, long hair floating about us in disarray in the soft breeze that remained with the evening.

I cleared my throat but did not move an inch.

She lifted her head. "Oh." Tucking her unruly hair back behind her ear, she met my gaze, but she didn't move other-

164

wise either. Her eyes were wide, but I couldn't tell if it was surprise, or relief, or amazement.

Having her so close, I couldn't help the rumble in my question. "Are you okay?"

Her fingers clenched against my chest, her thoughts churning once again. "It makes more sense now," she began, almost eagerly as if in gratification. "I was led to you in the first instance. It was you I'd been searching for all along."

My smile was tentative as I recalled the infuriating streak of jealousy I'd felt when we met Damien. "I'm glad."

Averting her gaze for a moment, her cheeks colored and her voice lowered with her next words. "I must admit, when we found Damien, I was...a bit disappointed." Then those sparkling violet eyes settled on mine once again. She didn't say it but I heard it.

I'd wanted it to be you.

I couldn't even speak. I was overwhelmed with a strange sort of pleasure.

Freyjn's gaze dropped to my mouth.

My heart hammered in my chest so hard, I was sure she could feel it. But I couldn't move. I was completely mesmerized.

It was no use.

Erin had been right before.

Freyjn was the one I'd been waiting for. Even when I thought she was a mere dream, I could never let her go. There was no one else for me except her.

Her breath warm on my cheek, she dipped her head lower...closer to mine.

That intoxicating scent surrounded me once again. Every inch of my skin thrummed with anticipation, with longing.

I felt like I'd waited years for this.

For her. For this one kiss.

That mysterious wind teased at her hair, swirling around us with her purple mist. She was so beautiful. I almost couldn't believe she was in my arms.

But then Freyjn stilled, her gaze flickering up to meet mine.

I blinked, sobering.

Was she second-guessing herself? Had she merely been caught up in the moment? Did she think I would reject her? She probably figured, much as I already had, that it wasn't a good idea for us to get more involved.

Except...

Desperate want stung my insides. I wanted to kiss her more than I wanted to breathe, more than I wanted to live. My chest heaved in suspense, in feverish anticipation. She needed to know how much she meant to me. How much the mere thought of losing her made me ache in ways I couldn't even articulate.

Her face remained hovering a few inches above mine.

So close...

I felt her move again. I wasn't sure if it was to get away or not. On impulse, I caught the nape of her neck, tugging her down to take her lips in mine.

Her surprised gasp stifled in my mouth.

As soon as our lips sealed together, a surge of warmth and electricity shot throughout my body—the immediate intensity of it almost blew my mind.

I squeezed my eyes shut as I breathed her in, and god bless her, Freyjn didn't pull away.

She melted against me. Her lips soft and sweet. The heat of her body reached out to envelop my entire being as ecstatic triumph filled my chest, crashing all over me, burying me deep in a world that consisted of only me and her.

Seconds stretched into minutes.

Heck, time could have been suspended altogether. I couldn't tell anymore.

This. This. This. My mind insisted. *I've been waiting for this. I've missed her. I love her. I've always loved her.*

I didn't understand my own thoughts, but then Freyjn let out a soft moan that stirred a different long-sleeping fire in my soul.

More...

Heart pounding in my ears, my fingers tangled in her silky hair as I pressed her closer to me. I slanted my head to kiss her again, deeper.

Freyjn broke off with a start. "Oh!"

Cold air rushed over my body as she quickly jumped up and was off of me in a split second. A good few feet away on the grass, she straightened up, smoothing down her hair and her clothes.

"Um." I rolled over to sit up on the ground. Self-conscious, I ran my fingers through my hair. "Did you... I-I shouldn't uh—"

Not looking at me, her face was red, those soft lips still full and plump.

From kissing me...

I almost groaned in my throat. It might have felt like forever, but suddenly it was nowhere near enough.

Ah, get a grip, Josh.

I shook my head briskly, my heart sinking to my stomach. Regret was written all over Freyjn's face. *Shoot.* I wanted to smack myself. I was so going to get reamed. Maybe Freyjn would finally blast me to oblivion with her freshly-recovered magic. Not to mention the imminent scolding from my dad if he found out what I'd just done.

Taking a deep breath, I was formulating the words to apologize when there was a weak moan of complaint from across the grassy lawn behind us.

"Ugh..." Still looking groggy, Damien had rolled onto his side, his face buried in his hands. "What the hell happened?"

22

Chapter Twenty-Two - Goodbyes

I slipped the postcard I'd bought from the boardwalk vendor through the mailbox slot. With my phone still conked out, I'd decided to just write my mom and sister a note to say goodbye. That way it would also take a few days before they were alerted to my being gone.

Then again, I wasn't entirely sure anyway if it was goodbye or not. Either way, I couldn't go all the way back home to bid everyone I knew farewell. There was no time to waste—or so I'd been told.

I stuck my hands in my pockets before walking toward the grassy lawn where Freyjn was preparing her magic to summon another portal, at the same time that my dad strolled down the paved path.

He'd used the last of his magic to obfuscate Damien's memories before putting him on the next subway to get back to his apartment, a mere one stop away. I'd even suggested that my dad make arrangements that would encourage Damien to move to California. With any hope, Damien would be able to live a relatively normal life now and find his real purpose.

Reaching me, my dad likewise stuffed his hands in his coat pockets as we walked along. "What did you tell your mom and sister?"

"That I was going on a long vacation, and that I'm hoping leaving my apartment for Erin to look after in the meantime is a good idea," I mused with a shrug. "Don't worry. I didn't mention how you've shockingly come back from the dead or that you're a magical warrior of sorts."

He chuckled.

Tilting my head, I gave his ghostly appearance a concerned once-over. Since exhausting his magic, his body indeed looked thinner, less solid, almost even translucent. "Dad, are you okay?"

My dad gave me a wan smile. "Here's another truth for you, Josh. I'm not really here."

I blinked in a startle. "What?"

"I'm not really here," he repeated. "I am merely the spirit of your father. He'd created me—with all his memories and emotions, when his human form could no longer keep the fight, and he imbued me with magic, just enough to ensure your survival. So there's really no need to go calling your mom and sister to let them know." He thumped on my shoulder. "I had solely existed for your protection. And now that your destiny is complete, my role is finished."

My jaw dropped, but there was also an ache in my chest once again.

My dad really was gone.

He slid an arm around my shoulder, his voice even lower than the developing quiet of the night. "I am sorry he wasn't there for you when he was alive. He struggled with all this, the inevitable destiny he knew was coming for us—for you." A shadow crossed his features. "He'd spent all that time planning, preparing, fighting to keep your existence a secret. Because he wanted you to live a normal life."

Despite the small smile breaking on his face, there was hesitation and a hint of fear there. "Did we do a good job?"

Dumb tears stung the corners of my eyes once again. I moved to throw my arms around my dad in understanding, appreciation. "Yes, Dad. You were great."

After a minute, I pulled away almost reluctantly. My chest was heavy with emotion. I was grateful at least to have had a second chance to spend time with my dad, if only in spirit, despite everything. Besides, he was the last person I had in my life here that I would see before I had to leave.

My dad cleared his throat as he straightened up. I could have sworn I also saw a sheen of tears in his eyes.

Yep. We were definitely alike in many ways.

My gaze drifted across the lawn toward Freyjn. She was doing more of those *Tai chi* motions with her hands. I didn't look at my dad when I asked, "I've met her before, haven't I?" in a low whisper so only he could hear.

I anticipated his response.

"I believe so."

And suddenly, everything made sense. No wonder Freyjn seemed so familiar. Whatever had happened during my 'nervous breakdown' years ago, when I was in the other realm, we had already met.

"How come she doesn't remember me?"

My dad's shoulders lifted. "I'm not sure. I think something happened in her world. Ironically, the only person who might know what had happened is you. Except, those memories were wiped."

"Can't you give me back my memories?"

He shook his head. "I can't. But," he paused in consideration, "in time, they may come back to you. Especially now that the magical block on you has been removed."

A bright spark of light came to life a few feet away from where Freyjn stood, the brilliance of the not-quite-liquid swirling silvery sphere flickering across our faces.

Blowing out a breath, I gave my dad a 'well, here goes nothing' look before walking over to Freyjn.

Upon my approach, her shoulders stiffened.

Oh, right. She hated me now.

I almost wished the ground would swallow me up instead. I wished I could assure her that whatever lapse in judgment that had happened earlier between us would never ever happen again. I took another step closer but she put her hand up first.

"Before we go, I...should tell you two things." Her tone was steady, authoritative, matter-of-fact.

But I wanted to apologize right away. "Look, I know I—"

She shook her head. "Stop—"

"Freyjn, please."

Wincing, she took a deep breath. "That's the first thing."

Nervous, I chewed on my bottom lip. "What?"

She paused for a long moment. "It's not my name."

What?

Narrowing my eyes, I recalled her hesitation when she was first asked for it at the diner. It struck me too that earlier she had spoken the name by accident as though she had been referring to someone else.

I *was* confused. But at the same time, for some reason, I felt as though I already knew. That persistent nagging deep in my gut I'd been ignoring for two days had insisted the name didn't suit her at all, to begin with.

I waited for her to say more, but she already looked uneasy enough. I didn't want to upset her or pressure her if she wasn't ready.

Tamping down the instant churn in my mind, the urge to figure everything out right now, I prompted instead, "What's the second thing?"

Another long pause.

"I am already betrothed."

That one felt like a punch in the gut.

My mouth dry, I was at a loss for words. "Oh."

Clearing her throat, she gave a quick wave to dismiss me again. "We must go now."

I balled my fists at my sides, trying to focus on the present once again. Neither the past nor the future mattered at the moment.

I was leaving.

I was leaving my world.

Freyjn (or whatever her name was) glanced back at me, a look halfway between wary and concerned in her eyes.

I looked past her toward the shimmery blue portal, steadily swirling away like a tear in reality, its consistent hum of magic whispering low over the sporadic crashing of waves along the boardwalk.

Turning back, I met the eyes of my dad's spirit. The crease on his forehead was also half-worried, but ultimately also half-resigned. I figured after everything, I was still going to be his son who always saw the best in any situation, including this one.

I cast a look around the Manhattan cityscape laid out before us, glanced up at the magical aura surrounding the Brooklyn Bridge, the dots of light from the rare small watercraft motoring up and down the East River, the handful of people enjoying their leisurely even stroll on the boardwalk.

Was this the last time I was ever going to see my world?

The pink fairy seemed to recognize my pause, understood it, respected it. She gave me all of twenty seconds before prompting, "Are you ready to go?"

It wasn't really a question.

But when I met those sparkling violet eyes once more, I realized I actually wasn't nervous at all.

I had absolutely no idea what was in store for me next—for us.

A new world. A new realm. A new responsibility I likely couldn't even fathom. I was meant to save an entire land.

But it was like what I'd already known before, deep in my soul.

I would do anything for this girl.

I would follow her anywhere.

Whatever happened next, as long as I was by her side, I would be content.

She lifted a delicate hand and held it out.

I took a deep breath...then took it in mine.

***

What lies ahead for Josh in the other realm? Will our Nameless Fay finally be named? Discover which questions about "Freyjn" will be answered in the next book of "The Dragons of Arcadia" series, where the extended world of the Land of Arcadia books picks up from.

Follow Josh and his nameless fairy on a sizzling, swoony epic fantasy romance adventure with Book 3 of The Dragons of Arcadia.

Welcome to the Land of Arcadia!

Do you like low-steam, thrilling, slow-burn, tension-filled fantasy romance?

The Curse of the Arcadian Stone: Nameless Fay is the full quadrilogy epilogue, three thousand years after S. R. Breaker's fantasy romance series **"The Dragons of Arcadia."** Discover the legend behind the curse by reading this thrilling, slow-burn epic fantasy romance now!

Reading order for all books in the extended world of the Land of Arcadia

Curse of the Dragon Heir (Book 1: The Dragons of Arcadia)

Arranged to the Fae Warrior (Book 1.5: The Dragons of Arcadia)

Reign of the Dragon Heir (Book 2: The Dragons of Arcadia)

The Curse of the Arcadian Stone (Book 1-3: Nameless Fay)

The Curse of the Arcadian Stone (Book 4: Nameless Fay/Book 2.5: The Dragons of Arcadia)

Flame of the Dragon Heir (Book 3: The Dragons of Arcadia)

Read on for a sneak peek at **Curse of the Dragon Heir, Book 1 of The Dragons of Arcadia series**.

Sneak Peek: Curse of the Dragon Heir

A headstrong Fae mage accidentally sets a mysterious evil demon free but he may be the key to unlocking her powers...

***

"Are you mated yet?" His voice was gruff but deeply rich.

Soleia shot him a glare. "That's none of your business."

The three warrior females exchanged looks.

Oh, great, Soleia thought in derision. Now they were probably going to start rumors about her and the demon. Just what she needed right now. "Thank you for your help." She dismissed the females with a wave before hanging up her cloak and turning back to fix her hair.

His scrutiny was unnerving her and also making her stomach do somersaults.

Stupid stomach. What the hell was wrong with her anyway? He was a cursed, dangerous demon that would destroy them all with one swish of his claws if given half the chance.

She cleared her throat, hurrying to finish grooming so she could exit the cramped indoor space, feeling a bit more cramped than before.

"Let me free."

Her eyebrows rose in incredulity at his words. "So you can kill me and everyone I know?"

He visibly swallowed hard. "I won't."

Soleia gave him a dull look. "Right."

His forehead creased in aggravation. "You don't even know who I am! How do you know it's justified to hold me against my will? How do you know you're not in the wrong here?"

"Look, the only wrong thing I did today was take too long at that dumb wraith forest. I should have ridden faster, fought harder. I should have just left some of the smaller wraiths alone. If I could have just put them to sleep, I could've—" She stopped short, blowing out a frustrated breath.

His eyes narrowed. "I thought you handled yourself quite well."

She gave him a deadpan look. "I know exactly what you're doing. You're trying to ply me with compliments so that I'll feel sorry for you or something and maybe release you from Oma's binding spell. But I'm not that dumb, Curse Boy."

He blinked like he didn't expect her to figure that out and he merely huffed in displeasure and looked away.

Soleia smirked. She was quite enjoying having so much power over him. "What kind of a dumb demon gets trapped on a tree anyway? And then to finally get free of the tree, only to get trapped by a necklace! Is this only the second curse that's been put on you? Or have there been more?"

That set him off.

He growled again, grabbing her by the shoulders and pinning her back against the wall.

She almost rolled her eyes at his futile intimidation efforts. Did he forget one word from her would send him doubling over? She met his gaze, undaunted. "You didn't scare me before. You definitely don't now."

He roared, leaning close to her face. He was clearly displeased, infuriated. "Mark my words," he rasped. "This spell *will* break. And when that time comes, I guarantee you, you *will* be scared. And then you will die."

"Right, whatever. But until then, Curse Boy, your life belongs to me." Soleia gave him a shove to push away but he pressed harder.

He was focused on her mouth. "Dathon," he growled. "My name is Dathon."

He spoke near her face. His freshly-showered scent was almost hypnotizing, overwhelming. Her chest heaved against his in her struggle to breathe and he must have noted her heart pounding. His incensed gaze seared into her.

Soleia blinked her senses back into focus and threw up her hands. "Fine!" And at her concession, he let her shrug him off. "Whatever."

* * *

Enjoyed the preview? Read **"Curse of the Dragon Heir"** now!

About the Author

S. R. BREAKER is a USA Today Bestselling Author of non-stop action adventure, offbeat YA/NA fantasy romance books. She lives in New Zealand with her husband and two kids. Suburban mum by day and author by night, she loves to live vicariously through her characters. They don't have to vacuum all day long and are almost always guaranteed to survive any fantastical or thrilling incidents, no matter how treacherous she writes them.

She likes binge-watching TV shows and reading books that take her to far enough unknown worlds—but then still have enough time to wash the dishes after.

Join her mailing list now and get a FREE e-book!

https://subscribe.breakerworlds.com/fantasy

Read on for a sneak peek of S. R. Breaker's Epic Fantasy Romance **The Secret of the Phoenix** (The Complete Phoenix Series)

Sneak Peek: The Secret of the Phoenix

"Always a dull moment" high school student Sarah Peters gets magically sent to another world. And now the bad guys with the big, scary robots want her dead. Enter tall, hot, and brooding Prince.

***

He grabbed my arm. "How do you know about the phoenix?"

"*Ow*," I said pointedly, loudly, and he dropped his hand. I gave him a fake gracious look. "Well, your stupid 'phoenix'," I relayed, motioning quotation marks with my fingers in mocking, "appeared in my bedroom, and the next thing I knew, I was here. You do the math."

"The stupid phoenix," he echoed, sounding offended, "is the insignia of my country."

"What country? Thailand?"

"Centeria."

"What?" I knew I sucked at geography but I was pretty sure I'd never heard of such a grandiose-sounding name for a country. "Where in the hell is that?"

"You have to come with me," he said, pulling me along behind him.

"*Ow*—stop grabbing me." I shrugged him off, exasperated. "Now, I'm not going anywhere until I get some answers here," I declared.

He had started to groan when he paused, his gaze halfway to the sky. "I have a feeling you'll be changing your mind."

I shot him a wry look. "Yeah, sure."

Then I heard what sounded like an explosion from behind me and looked over in time to see a huge black and indigo robot crash through two building structures. The ground shook and I held on to the wall. "What the—?" My jaw dropped as I recognized the robot from the vision I'd seen this afternoon on the street, just as the thing seemed to look over and point a mechanical arm weapon in our direction—in *my* direction.

A shot fired and hit the top of the structure above us and debris crashed down. I jumped aside and to the ground. "—the hell?" I asked, gawking up at the thing.

"Change your mind yet?"

No time to answer, I scrambled up and started running down the street again. I looked around, baffled. I'd watched enough television to figure that robots were supposed to fight other robots. But these ones seemed to be chasing us—not anyone or anything else. *This has to be the stupidest dream in the entire world!*

***

Enjoyed the preview? **The Secret of the Phoenix** is only available on Amazon.com

Jump into a fast-paced, easy-to-read portal fantasy sci-fi adventure across parallel worlds with S. Breaker's recently completed YA series **Selfless**.

"They're after you. But which you...?"

Mistaken for her imperiled, notorious genius alternate self, Laney's accidental trip to a parallel world could very quickly turn very deadly.

Read on for a sneak peek...

Sneak Peek: The Selfless Series

They're after you. But which you…? Mistaken identities. Parallel worlds. Government conspiracies. Out of time. Save the multiverse. Save yourself. Don't get erased. Ready?

***

"Did we lose them yet?" Laney rubbed her hands over her arms in the freezing cold.

Noah looked intently at the gadget on his arm, tapping a few keys seemingly in mid-air. "I wouldn't count on it."

The rain had abated but it was still dark. It seemed like they had run deeper into the city. She still didn't know where the hell they were.

The whole city was deserted. Old-fashioned cars were stopped in the middle of the streets, some having crashed onto other cars, or onto building facades with faded, cracked brickwork, fallen tarnished bicycles dotted the road, a vaguely iconic-looking red double-decker bus lay on its side at the far end of the street, almost out of view. There was no trace of any other people around, not even animals.

Several doors to apartment buildings across the street had been left wide open. It was as though everyone had dropped everything to leave in a hurry.

"What...happened here?" she wanted to know, half-dreading the answer to her question.

"This is the dead city. Ground zero."

"Ground zero. For what?"

He sighed then as if it was no big deal, he relayed, "The global cascade bomb that nearly obliterated all organic life on our world sixty-seven years ago."

"Th-the *what*?" Laney gasped in shock, horrified.

He shot her a slightly annoyed look. "Look, can you keep up? We've already missed the rendezvous window and we're nowhere near where we need to be.

Laney braced her hands on her knees, still trying to catch her breath, and shot him an annoyed look right back. "Hey, we've been running all night. I don't know about the Laney from your world but *this* one is not a triathlon champion."

He didn't respond to her statement. "Come on." He motioned, leading them through a gap in the broken wire fence surrounding a construction site.

"You didn't answer my question earlier," Laney spoke up. "That guy, the one who tried to kill me the other night. He was looking for something. What is it anyway?"

Noah shot her a look, hesitating. "Do you know what spacetime is?"

"Of course," Laney replied dismissively.

He narrowed his eyes at her, dubious.

She blinked again. "I mean," she began. "I know it's like a *science* thing."

"Spacetime is the fabric of the multiverse within which all our worlds exist," he stated as if he was talking to a child. "Do you know what a wormhole is?"

She pursed her lips.

"What do you learn in school?" he asked in disbelief.

She made another face. "Once again," she said, gesturing to herself from top to bottom. "Normal person. *Not* genius nerd."

Noah rolled his eyes. "Look, the main thing is, there's a device. It makes it possible for a person to move back and forth between two distinct realities."

"Okay."

Noah blinked hard. "No. *Not okay.* What they're ignoring is the probability that this device is going to cause a break in the spacetime continuum, effectively erasing us all from existence. And life as we know it will be over. *Everywhere.*"

Laney mused, "I still don't understand what any of this has to do with me."

"Well, obviously, the government bureaucracies in my world really want this device back—badly. And unfortunately, they think *you* have it."

She stifled an incredulous laugh. "Why the heck would they think *that*?"

"Because...you created it, Laney."

✳✳✳

Enjoyed the preview? **The Selfless Series** is available to purchase at your favorite online bookstore.